SHE WAS A PRO AT THREE-CARD MONTE, BUT THE GAME SHE PLAYED BEST WAS FOR THE HIGHEST STAKES OF ALL....

Lita lifted off the three top cards and spread them out. Foxx saw that he had to choose between the three of hearts, the ace of spades, and the king of clubs. Unhesitatingly, he tapped the black ace.

"You must be a very brave man," Lita said as she began to strip-shuffle the three cards.

"What gives you that idea?"

"Because you have chosen to make your bet on the card of death."

FOXX!

A bold new hero in the Old West.
Don't miss his previous adventures:

FOXX!
FOXX'S GOLD
FOXX HUNTING
FOXX'S HERD

FOXX'S VIXEN

Zack Tyler

A DELL BOOK

Published by
Dell Publishing Co., Inc.
1 Dag Hammarskjold Plaza
New York, New York 10017

Copyright © 1982 by Context, Inc.

All rights reserved. No part of this book may be reproduced or transmitted in any form or by any means, electronic or mechanical, including photocopying, recording or by any information storage and retrieval system, without the written permission of the Publisher, except where permitted by law.

Dell ® TM 681510, Dell Publishing Co., Inc.

ISBN: 0-440-12781-5

Printed in the United States of America
First printing—March 1982

FOXX'S VIXEN

CHAPTER 1

Outside the railroad coach the guns had been silent for several moments. Bright orange-red streaks of muzzle flash no longer stabbed the night's blackness. Foxx listened to the fading hoofbeats of the night riders fading to silence, but did not move. He wanted to be absolutely sure that what he interpreted as the attackers' retreat was not just a ruse by the raiders to lure those in the car to show a light and reveal themselves once again.

Even when the thudding hooves of the night riders' mounts no longer reached his ears, Foxx waited. Standing up, he peered into the velvet-black night of the Arizona desert country. On this side of the car he saw nothing but the star-studded sky, but when he turned to look through the shattered glass of the car windows, he could see distant pinpricks of light from the bobbing lanterns carried by men rushing toward the car.

"I guess they're gone, all right," he told his companions at last. "We might as well light the lamps again."

Suiting action to his words, Foxx struck a match and reached for the chain of the main lamp, which was fixed to the ceiling in the center of the coach. He held the chain down until the sputtering of acetylene gas from the tank became a steady hissing, and by standing on tiptoe and stretching high, Foxx touched the twin mantles with the match flame. The mantles glowed green for a second or two before steadying down into a dazzling white light, setting off the interior of Caleb Petersen's private car in harsh relief.

Before blowing out the match, Foxx took one of his crooked Italian fisherman's stogies out of his vest pocket and lighted it. He looked around at the interior of the private car through the cloud of acrid blue smoke that wreathed his head.

Caleb Petersen, president of the Chicago & Kansas Railroad, had been kneeling between the two windows across the car from Foxx. He was getting to his feet a bit unsteadily, blinking his eyes in the sudden brightness.

Clara Petersen and Vida Martin were still trying to get themselves untangled from the legs of the dinner table. Caleb went to help them get to their feet.

"Who the devil was that shooting at us?" he asked.

"Whoever it was, they wasn't real serious about it," Foxx said coolly. "They'd be here yet if they'd meant business."

Foxx had wasted no time when the first shot sounded outside the car. He'd thrust the women under the table in one swift fluid motion before reaching for the lamp chain and yanking it down, plunging the coach into the protection of total darkness.

By that time the brittle noise of shattering glass was filling the air as bullets from the night riders' guns crashed through the windowpanes and thunked into the walls of Caleb's luxurious private car.

"I'd like to know who it was, myself," Foxx went on. "And I'll sure make it my business to find out."

Foxx was giving most of his attention to the revolver he still held. He'd already ejected the cases of the spent cartridges and was fishing fresh ammunition from an inner pocket of his coat and shoving it through the loading gate of the Colt Cloverleaf revolver.

He went on, "I don't imagine they'll come back, whoever it was, but if they do . . ."

He let his words trail off into silence as he revolved the cylinder of the compact, stubby-barreled pistol to bring the chambers into line outside the frame, which flattened their swell to the width of a man's hand. Then he thumbed the hammer to lock the cylinder at half-cock before restoring the weapon to the holster-pocket sewn into the inside breast of his coat, where the slight bulge it made was hidden by the coat's full-cut lapel.

Foxx had not belted on his Smith & Wesson American before leaving his stateroom for dinner and was feeling as sorry now as he had when the surprise attack started that he hadn't put on the long-barreled .38. By habit, though, he'd tucked his Colt Cloverleaf into its usual place, and when the first shots sounded from the night, the little revolver had been in his hand even before he'd kicked away his chair and leaped from the table.

Foxx had emptied the four chambers of the Cloverleaf, snap-shooting at the dimly visible silhouettes of the night riders. He'd known that his shooting was nothing but token resistance, a threatening gesture to keep the attacking force from coming too near the car. Even if he'd been able to see a target, the stubby Colt lacked the range to reach the horsemen, who'd kept their distance from the coach while peppering it with their rifles.

Clara and Vida were now on their feet, looking around the car, still somewhat dazed by the suddenness with which the night riders had stolen up, carried out their attack, and vanished into the darkness.

Foxx moved to Vida's side. He wanted to take her in his arms and soothe the troubled frown off her face but knew that to do so openly in front of Clara and Caleb would be unwise. Vida was sure that her older sister and brother-in-law had a pretty shrewd idea that she and Foxx were enjoying more than just a casual friendship, but Caleb's straitlaced ideas made discussion of their relationship impossible.

"Are you all right?" Foxx asked, directing his question as much to Clara as to Vida.

Vida said, "I—I suppose so. I don't hurt anywhere, except my knee, where I hit it on something when you were getting us under the table."

"That was the safest place I could think of for you ladies to be," Foxx said. "And there wasn't any time to lallygag, not with lead already flying."

"I should think there wasn't!" Clara agreed,

smoothing her hair. "Not only lead but glass! Just look at those windows!"

"I'm not worrying about the windows." Caleb frowned, his eyes moving along the pocked walls. "They can be replaced in the shop here while we're gone. But that matched walnut paneling is another thing! Replacing it is going to be a real job!"

Foxx suppressed a smile. He'd witnessed people under stress too many times to count, and he knew their reactions were unpredictable. Some would go to pieces, others would retreat into a state of silent, staring shock, and some would fix their attention on the most trivial matters possible to keep their minds from dwelling on the dangers they'd escaped.

He followed Caleb and Clara and Vida in surveying the damage done to the coach's interior. The private car which was Caleb's pride had only recently been delivered from George Pullman's railroad coach works in the East. As with most cars of its type, a combined parlor and dining area took up two thirds of its space. The galley was at the rear of the coach, with sleeping quarters behind it for a cook and helper. Four staterooms filled the front end, two on each side, each stateroom provided with its own tiny bath. A narrow corridor between the staterooms led to the front vestibule.

At the moment the car was a shambles. Broken glass glittered on the carpeted floor. Bullets had torn through the wooden exterior walls of the car leaving bright vertical scars in the richly glowing walnut paneling, and where the slugs had passed across the coach and entered the opposite wall there were ugly black pockmarks. The liquor cabinet built into the galley had been struck more than once, and a strong smell of wine and spirits was beginning to fill the air as the contents of the broken bottles trickled out and seeped into the carpet.

Voices from outside halted the conversation in the car. One of the approaching men shouted, "Anybody hurt in there, Mr. Petersen?"

"No one was hit," Caleb called back. "But we'll need some help to clean up the mess in here."

"It's all right if I come in, then?" the man asked.

Foxx had recognized the voice, and when Caleb looked at him, he nodded and said, "That's Wade Benton, Caleb. The yardmaster."

"Come in, Benton," Caleb called.

Benton swung up the vestibule steps and into the car. He was a short, compact man, wearing a dark suit. He carried a switchman's lantern in one hand, a heavy Colt Navy revolver in the other.

"I got my men here as soon as I could," he apologized to Caleb. "They was all scattered out, though, and I guess I just couldn't gather 'em up fast enough to be much help."

"Don't worry about it," Caleb told him. "The men who staged that attack were here and gone before we really knew what was happening."

Benton looked at the shattered windows and bullet-pocked walls of the private car for a moment, then shook his head and said, "You're lucky, I guess, Mr. Petersen. If I'd thought for a minute something like this would happen, I'd've had the men spot your car on a siding closer to the depot."

"It's not your fault, Benton," Caleb replied. "We wanted to be as far away from the depot and the roundhouse as we could get, but I can see now that it was a mistake."

Foxx said to Benton, "I thought you told me when we pulled in that you hadn't had any trouble here in La Paz for the last two months."

"And we haven't, Mr. Foxx," the yardmaster replied, a worried frown creasing his broad face. "They've let us alone so long that we've sorta got out of the habit of keeping our guard up, I suppose. We ain't been bothered here since the railhead's pushed east, into the foothills. But you know how much trouble Pat Riley has had up there."

"About the same kind of thing we just went through?" Foxx asked.

Benton nodded. "Pretty much. A bunch of night riders show up out of nowheres and let off a few rounds and then get away as fast as they came. But we've lost a few men, just the same."

"Including two of my detectives," Foxx said grimly.

"Yes, sir," Benton agreed. "But you'd know all about that, I guess."

"Not as much as I intend to know," Foxx replied.

Caleb broke in. "You'd better get a couple of your men to clean up the worst of this mess in the car here, Benton," he said to the yardmaster. "Don't try to do too much. Tai Sun will take care of whatever your crew can't handle tonight. I let him off to go into town after he'd finished cooking our dinner. But have your men clean up the broken glass, and nail some boards over those broken windows as soon as you can."

"Right away, Mr. Petersen," Benton replied. "I'll stay on hand to see they do a good job for you." He looked at the car's interior. "If you folks would like to get out of the car while they're cleaning up, I'll have a yard mule spot a day coach right behind you on the siding."

"I'd rather stay right here, Caleb," Clara Petersen said to her husband. "We'll just go into our staterooms to get out of the way while they're taking care of things."

"While we're waiting, I'll step outside and have a look around," Foxx told them. "I'll talk to the men who was working in the yards, see if any of 'em can tell me which way them night riders come from, what direction they taken when they left. I'll keep an eye on the car while I'm out there and be back as soon as Benton's men are finished."

Before going outside, Foxx stepped into his stateroom and donned his pistol belt. He took a lantern from the cubby between the staterooms and the vestibule door and swung down the steps to the cinder-covered ground. None of Benton's crew was in sight, though two of them were already at work inside the private car. Foxx decided that the yardmaster had sent the others to get boards and tools with which to cover the windows, and he began circling the car, widening the diameter of his circle as he moved.

A thin, chilling wind was blowing off the Bill Williams River, less than a mile from the southern edge of La Paz. Foxx turned up his coat collar to take the edge off its bite. He'd made three sweeps around the car before he spotted the first cartridge case, its fresh brass gleaming brightly on the cindered ground. He stopped and picked it up.

Foxx brought the open end of the case to his nose.

The smell of burned powder was still strong. He held it close to the lantern to examine the brass more carefully. The figure ".41" was stamped on its rimmed bottom, and even in the uncertain lantern light Foxx could see on its sides the four dimples that marked it as having been fired from a sleeved-down Lebel, the rifle that had been brought by tens of thousands into Mexico a dozen years earlier by the occupying armies of Napoleon III.

Tossing the case aside, Foxx continued his search until he'd picked up and inspected three more cases. One was from a Civil War Springfield, one from a Martini-Henry, and the third was a twin to the first one he'd picked up.

"Apaches or Mexicans, or maybe a mix-up of the two," Foxx mused as he trudged over the rough earth of the yards. "Which don't lead to much I hadn't already figured out. And it's a long ways from telling me why, which is what I got to know before I can get to the bottom of things."

Two of Benton's men were nailing boards over the broken windows of Caleb's car when Foxx returned. Benton was standing a little distance from the car, supervising the job.

"I noticed you looking around the yard," he said to Foxx. "Don't guess you found anything useful, did you?"

"Nothing but a few cartridge cases. From the looks of them, I'd say most of the bunch that hit us tonight was Apaches or Mexicans. The cases were from old guns, the kind you'd look for a ragtag-bobtail outfit to be carrying."

"About what I expected." The yardmaster nodded.

"This bunch tonight was just like the ones that used to plague us before the railhead got so far east. Now they're bothering Pat Riley up at the construction camp."

"You're sure it's the same bunch?" Foxx asked.

"It's got to be. They ride in like tonight, shoot things up, and ride off before we can do anything to stop 'em."

"You must've chased after 'em a few times," Foxx suggested.

"Well, now, Mr. Foxx, the men we hire on construction don't always feel they owe the road enough to take on a shooting fight. They sorta figure it's outside of the jobs they was hired for. And most of the ones I've hired on for my yard crew are new, and they mostly feel the same way right now."

"Oh, I can see that." Foxx nodded. "But you always had some of Jim Flaherty's policemen or one of the men from my detective force here. They're paid to handle trouble. What about them?"

"Well, the policemen all moved up with the railhead. Your detectives tried to set traps for the night riders, but they always seemed to know when a trap was waiting and stayed away. And both of your detectives went up to the railhead with the idea of hiding out at the edge of the camp and trailing the bastards back to where they'd come from. That's how your men got killed."

"I'd intended to wait until tomorrow to talk to you about them two men outa my force that got killed," Foxx said. "But seeing as how we've got nothing better to do right now, suppose you tell me what happened to them. The reports I got from the division super didn't give me a lot to go on."

"I don't know that I could do much better," Benton said somewhat hesitantly. "They worked under the super, you know."

"Sure. But he's down in Mexico, fixing up things so that Mr. Petersen's trip will be easier, so I can't talk to him for a while. Anything you can think of might help me a lot."

"Like I said, I don't know too much. It happened up at the railhead, but Pat Riley told me your men was hiding out, the way they'd planned to, ready to follow the raiders."

"Does anybody know for sure that's what they did?"

"Well, they must have," Benton replied. "All anybody really knows, I guess, is that they turned up dead. Both times the body was found tied to stakes out at the edge of the yards a couple of days after them night riders had hit us."

"Now, that's something I hadn't heard about." Foxx frowned. "Frank Sanders didn't mention anything special about their bodies being mishandled, just said they'd been found."

There was a shudder in Benton's voice as he went on, "I'll tell you something right now, Mr. Foxx. I guess I'm as loyal to the C&K as anybody else that's been working for it awhile, but I can't say I'd blame anybody for being edgy after they heard about what happened to your detectives."

"Maybe you better explain that," Foxx said.

"Well, I already told you part of it, about them being tied up to long stakes that somebody'd drove into the ground out at the edge of the yards. But both of them men had been stripped bare naked." Benton looked at the darkness outside the circle of light cast by the workmen's lanterns and dropped his voice to a half-whisper as he went on, "Their peckers and balls had been cut off, and they had cuts all over, like somebody'd hacked at 'em for a while. And on top of that, they'd been scalped. Their heads was just one big mess of blood with the bone showing through."

"Sounds to me like Apache work," Foxx said, as much to himself as to Benton. "Or somebody that wanted it to look like Apaches had been at 'em."

"That's what some of my men said, Apache torture," Benton told Foxx. "I wouldn't know, though. I didn't get out here to the West until after the Indians were pretty much tamed. At least they was in the places I worked at. But the signs on the bodies was in Spanish."

"Signs? What signs, Benton? You mean paper signs with words on 'em, I guess, not footprints or what a tracker would call signs."

"Yes, sir. Both of your men had a piece of paper pegged on their chest, with words on it."

"Nobody's mentioned any signs to me before now," Foxx said.

"Well, they were there, all right, because I saw 'em. The signs read the same, both times, 'NO PASE EL FERROCARIL.'" Benton paused after struggling through the unfamiliar words, then went on, "Some of my crewmen know Spanish, and they told me that means, 'The railroad ain't going to go no further,' or words to that effect."

Foxx nodded thoughtfully. He'd learned a bit of Spanish from his youth with the Comanches. To them, it had been almost a second language, an inheritance dating back almost two centuries, to the time when the first colonists settled in New Mexico. During the years when the Indians traded chiefly with the new colonies, Spanish had become a lingua franca of the tribes whose traditional territories bordered the settlements, not only of the Comanches but of the Apaches, Pawnees, Kiowas, Navahos, and the Pueblo people.

He asked Benton, "These signs, did they show up on any of the other men that's been killed along the C&K right of way?"

"Not that I've heard of," the yardmaster replied. "But your detectives are the only ones I know about that tried to follow the night riders to wherever they hide out at."

Before Foxx could frame another question, the men working on the window-boarding job stopped hammering and began gathering up their tools and the pieces of scrap lumber left over from the repair work. Foxx could tell that the yardmaster wanted to get his men back to their regular jobs.

"I do thank you for your help, Benton," he said. "Chances are I'll be looking for you again tomorrow to ask whatever questions pop into my mind after I do some thinking about what you just been telling me."

Inside, Caleb's private car looked strange, with its windows replaced by raw wood, its polished walnut paneled walls scarred by bullet holes. Caleb saw Foxx looking at the damage and managed a half-smile.

"I suppose the damage to the walls can be repaired," he said. "It'll have to wait until I get the car back to San Francisco, of course."

"Now, stop worrying, Caleb!" Clara said scoldingly. "None of us was hurt, and these days almost anything that gets broken or scarred up can be repaired."

Vida seconded her sister. "Clara's right, you know. From the way those bullets were pouring in here, I think we got off very lightly indeed."

"Oh, I agree with both of you," Caleb said. "But what puzzles me is why we were attacked at all. It certainly wasn't an attempt to rob us, or those men would've been quieter."

"They didn't set out to rob," Foxx said. "They come here to do just what they did, shoot up your car. Oh, I'd guess if one of us had been hurt or even killed, they wouldn't've minded, but my bet is that all they was looking to do was try to throw a scare into you, Caleb."

"That must mean you learned something new while you were out looking around."

"I found out a few things, mostly by accident, but not about who done the shooting." Foxx paused long enough to light one of his crooked stogies, then said almost casually, "Frank Sanders didn't send a very good report of them earlier night-rider shootings back to San Francisco, Caleb. If I'd found out from them reports what I picked up accidental-like tonight, I'd have been here a long time ago."

"I don't follow you, Foxx," Caleb said with a puzzled frown. "I read Frank's reports, too, you know. As far as I could tell, he covered all the essential facts."

"All but the one that explains why there was any attacks at all," Foxx replied.

"Maybe you'd better explain," Caleb said.

Foxx told the others what he'd learned from Wade Benton. He omitted only the details of the genitals that had been cut off the dead detectives, sparing nothing in relating the scalping and stab wounds and knife slashes which had mutilated the bodies. When he'd finished, Caleb shook his head with a worried frown.

"I just can't understand why Frank didn't mention all those details," he said. "Unless he was afraid I'd think he wasn't doing a competent job and replace him as division superintendent, which I just might've done, after the second killing."

"From what Benton told me, there's been more than just two killings since these attacks began," Foxx added. "He mentioned that there's been more men killed, the times them night riders have shot up the construction camp up at the railhead. I don't seem to recall seeing that in any of Sanders's reports that Jim Flaherty's passed on to me."

"Are you sure Benton knows what he is saying?" Caleb asked.

"I just got through talking to him," Foxx replied tartly. "And as far as I know, there ain't a thing wrong with him. Now, it ain't just mischief that's behind all of this, Caleb. I got a feeling there's a lot more to it than just a bunch of local badmen. And I aim to run whoever it is to the earth, if it's the last thing I do!"

CHAPTER 2

"Now, just hold on to your temper," Caleb told Foxx. "I wasn't suggesting Benton was wrong. I was just surprised because Frank didn't mention any other killings before the first of your detectives was murdered. All he sent from the railhead was Pat Riley's figures on the trackage laid. If he'd mentioned killings, you and Jim would've gotten copies of those reports."

"There's something real wrong someplace along the line, then," Foxx said soberly, his burst of anger fading.

"I'd hate to think the fault's with Frank Sanders." Caleb's brows pulled together. "He's been with the C&K from the very start. And I knew him a long time before there was a single foot of track laid for the Chicago & Kansas. No, I can't believe Frank would hold anything back from me, Foxx."

Just then Clara Petersen interrupted them, before Foxx had a chance to ask Caleb the question that had popped into his mind. "Vida and I made a fresh pot of coffee while the yard crew was boarding up the windows. Now, before you start making speeches, Caleb, let's all sit down and have something to calm our nerves."

"It's going to take a little more than coffee to do that, Clara," Caleb told his wife. "You get the coffee, and I'll get some brandy to go with it, if there's an unbroken bottle left in the cabinet."

"While you're looking, you might see if they missed one of them bottles of Cyrus Noble," Foxx suggested. "That'd suit my taste a lot better'n brandy does."

During the few minutes that passed while the four were settling down at the table, Foxx had time to cool off. He lighted a fresh stogie and sipped the smooth bourbon before he brought up what had occurred to him during the pause.

"I wasn't meaning to point my finger at Frank Sanders," he told Caleb. "Them reports he sends in to you goes through a lot of other people's hands before you get 'em, Caleb."

"I was just thinking the same thing," Caleb nodded. "They'd be handled by the telegrapher here at La Paz, the one at our main station in San Francisco, and then by the one at our office downtown. Any one of them could tamper with Frank's messages."

"Even worse than that," Foxx reminded him, "every brass-pounder along our line keeps his key open all the time. It'd be real simple for one of 'em to break the circuit to San Francisco, maybe change a message or cut something out of it. Then he'd just send it on, and nobody'd be any wiser."

"He could, of course." Caleb frowned. "It'd be awfully hard to catch up with a trick of that kind, wouldn't it, Foxx? You wouldn't know where to start looking for the man who's responsible."

"I thought all your confidential messages were sent in code, Caleb," Clara interrupted.

"Codes ain't all that hard to break," Foxx pointed out. He sipped his whiskey, gazing over the glass at Caleb, and promised, "Soon as I get free from this job here, I'll start looking, and I won't stop till I find whoever it is that's selling us out."

For a moment Caleb frowned worriedly, then he said, "Just as a guess, you'll probably find he's a spy hired by Holliday's crowd, or by Huntington and Stanford. The Santa Fe and the Southern Pacific want to be the first to open up a southern line to the East, just like we do."

"I had them in my mind, too." Foxx nodded. "They sure ain't going to set on their hands and let us alone while we push our iron east right between their lines."

"There's one thing bothering me, Foxx," Caleb went on. "If either one of them has put a spy in the C&K, they'll know by now that I'm going to Mexico. Maybe—" He stopped and shook his head, then said, "No. Keeping track moving east from La Paz is a lot more important than my Mexico idea."

Vida said, "Clara's told me a little bit about your plan for a line down in Mexico, Caleb, but I still don't understand it. They have railroads down there already, don't they?"

"Of course. But I'm not thinking about pushing C&K rails into Mexico from the north, Vida. I just want to build a short line, a hundred and fifty miles of track across the narrowest part of southern Mexico, from a port called Minatitlán on the Gulf of Mexico to another port on the Pacific, Juichitan."

"But what earthly use would the C&K have for a hundred-and-fifty-mile railroad so far from your main lines?" Vida frowned.

"For handling freight shipments between the Atlantic Coast and California. I've done a lot of figuring, and I'm convinced a line of that kind can be a real money-maker for us."

"But when I came West, Caleb, I traveled all the way on railroads and only had to change trains four times."

"You weren't a freight shipment, though, Vida." Caleb smiled. "What the Burlington and Rock Island and Union Pacific and Southern Pacific call the Iowa Pool took care of you, but it doesn't move freight as fast it does passengers."

"It does handle freight, doesn't it?" she asked.

"Of course it does," Caleb replied. "But it's slow and expensive. Now, if we take cargo off a steamship at Minatitlán, haul it overnight to Juichitan, then load it on another steamship, we can lay down freight in San Francisco in about the same time it'd take to ship it cross-country by rail, and for a lot less money, even allowing the C&K a good profit."

"Well, I suppose you know a lot more about these things than I do," Vida said.

"Of course he does!" Clara told her sister proudly. "But I think you and I had better go to bed now, Vida, and let Caleb and Foxx talk business. And goodness knows I'm ready for bed!"

"You've been right closemouthed about this scheme you was explaining to Vida," Foxx said after the women had said their good-nights and gone to their staterooms. "I hadn't heard a word from anybody about it, until now. Of course, it ain't exactly in my department—"

"If it was anything else, I wouldn't've been so secretive," Caleb told Foxx. "Jared Blossom's the only one in the office I've talked with about it, though. Even Frank Sanders doesn't know why he's in Mexico arranging this trip. I didn't want any talk about the Mexico idea until I've got Diaz's approval on the franchise for that road across the isthmus."

"I can see why," Foxx said. "Well, I sure won't say a word, Caleb, even if there was anybody down here in Arizona Territory to talk about it. Hell's bells, I got my hands full as it is, running down that spy we was talking about a few minutes ago."

"Well, I'm sure you'll find him, but I'm afraid it won't be in time to stop the word from getting out."

"I can let this job here go and begin looking for him right away," Foxx suggested.

Caleb shook his head. "No. Finishing the line to the East is as important to the C&K as the Mexico plan. Maybe more so."

"Whatever you say, Caleb."

For a moment the C&K president looked at Foxx thoughtfully, then he said, "I suppose you might as well know why, but I'll ask you not to talk with anybody about what I'm going to tell you." When Foxx nodded, Caleb went on, "Right now, we're in pretty deep water because of the money panic in the East. It's going to take awhile for you to uncover that spy, and I don't have all the time I'd like to maneuver in."

"I never paid much mind to all that panic talk," Foxx said. "I just figured the C&K was doing pretty good."

"We are. We could go on operating on the trackage we've got now and make money. Not a lot of money, but enough to handle our payrolls and give the stockholders a little dividend every year. Compared to the other Western roads, though, we're still pretty small potatoes, because we got such a late start. Getting our rails into Kansas by this southern route will even things up. That's why it's so important to break the bottleneck we've got at the railhead."

"I hadn't heard about that," Foxx said.

"Probably because I've told everybody to keep quiet about it. But we can't lay rail any faster or further until the bridge over the Santa Maria River is finished."

"And even if it does get finished, Pat Riley sure ain't going to push iron fast until I get them night riders corralled." Foxx nodded. "Well, I wouldn't worry too much, Caleb. Bridges got a way of being stubborn, but they do get finished."

"There's more to it than that," Caleb said. "We need the government subsidy money, too. So far, we've been building over flatland, and that's only a sixteen-thousand-dollar subsidy for every mile of track we lay. Now that we're in the foothills, the subsidy's doubled, thirty-two thousand a mile. As soon as we get east of the Santa Maria River and hit the mountains, it goes up to forty-eight thousand. That's over and above the twenty sections of land a mile, of course, which we'll sell off as fast as we can."

Foxx whistled. "That's a lot of cash, Caleb. I never paid much attention to how them subsidies add up, before now."

"I'm counting pretty heavily on Riley holding down our costs on this eastern line, so that we'll have the spare cash we need to build the Mexico line," Caleb explained. "If he can just keep the rails pushing east, it'll be clear sailing."

"You don't have to draw me any pictures," Foxx said. "What you want is for me to stop them raids that's slowing up Riley's construction eastward before I begin looking for that spy."

"That's about the size of it." Caleb nodded. "So you stay here in La Paz when we leave tomorrow, Foxx. We won't be gone long, three weeks at most."

"Seems to me that's going to make you cover a lot of ground in a mighty short while."

"It shouldn't be a hard trip, from what Frank Sanders has found out, and we'll have Tai Sun along to take care of us. We'll take a steamboat just above the mouth of the Colorado, meet Frank at a little port called Ocampo. Then we go across the mountains in a carriage for about sixty miles and travel the rest of the way to Mexico City by train. The trip will take a week going and coming, and if I can't get that franchise out of Diaz in the week we'll be there, I won't get it at all."

"Well, I wish you luck," Foxx said.

Caleb nodded. "Thanks." He stood up and stretched. "I'd better go before Clara comes out and drags me off to bed."

"I'm aiming to stay up and wait for Magruder to come back," Foxx said. "I sorta looked for him before now. I sent him to town to nose around a little bit, and he ought to've heard about the night riders by now and be hustling back."

"You're going to send him up to the railhead to be on hand if the raiders hit our construction camp, I suppose?"

"No, Caleb. I'm going to send him down to Mexico with you."

"Now, hold on, Foxx!" Caleb protested. "I don't need one of your men as a bodyguard! I can look after myself."

"I'll tell you what you told me a little while ago, Caleb. Don't go getting riled up. If you'll just stop and think about it a minute, you'll recall you've been a target before, only that time it was a young boy that got to you right in your own house. This time, it's a gang, and you're going to be in places you don't know anything about."

Foxx didn't think it was necessary to remind Caleb that he'd been the one who'd foiled that attempt on the C&K president's life.

"Just the same—" Caleb began.

Foxx brushed the interruption aside. He went on, "Now, ever since I finally figured out we got a spy someplace in the C&K, I been thinking what a prime target you'd be in Mexico. It wasn't no accident that bunch shot up this car tonight. They knew you was here, and they tried to get you. I'm betting they won't give up, either. And if I don't send Magruder along, it'll just be you and Clara and Vida and Sanders and

Tai Sun against a gang that can hit you any time they feel like it."

"But you brought Magruder along to replace the men from your detective force"—Caleb's voice trailed off into a thoughtful silence as he finished—"who were killed a few weeks ago."

"As long as I'm here to take care of things myself, I can do without Magruder," Foxx pointed out. "Now, I know you ain't afraid, but think about Clara and Vida. I don't expect you'd want them to get hurt, just because they was with you."

"Of course not!" Caleb replied indignantly. Then he threw up his hands and added, "All right, Foxx. You've persuaded me Magruder goes along. Now I'm going to bed. We'll make whatever plans we need to in the morning."

Foxx smoked another of his twisted black stogies and sipped at the Cyrus Noble until Magruder arrived, a quarter of an hour later. A former San Francisco police detective, Magruder was one of the newest additions to the C&K's detective force, which was under Foxx's command.

Magruder reported that no one in La Paz seemed to be upset about the attack on the Petersen car, that he'd known nothing about it until a few minutes earlier. He'd overheard someone in a saloon casually mention the night riders and had hurried back to the yards. He listened carefully while Foxx gave him instructions on his changed assignment, and went to bed.

Foxx took a final swallow of whiskey and went into his own stateroom. He'd stripped off his clothes and was washing his hands and face at the tiny lavatory when the door opened and Vida Martin slipped inside.

"I thought you and Caleb would never finish talking," she said, closing the door softly and keeping her voice just above a whisper. "Didn't you know I'd want to come and be with you tonight, Foxx?"

"I was hoping you would."

Vida's soft, wavy hair swept down to place her lustrous eyes and full, moist lips in a shining frame of copper red. She wore a thin, clinging negligee of ivory-hued chiffon. The translucent material dropped from the garment's high neck to her full breasts and sloped down over the twin globes, the outline of their dark-pink rosettes visible through the fabric each time she moved. The symmetry of their swell was broken by the budding tips in the center of each of the rosettes, twin dots forming reversed dimples in the soft chiffon.

Foxx finished drying his hands, dropped the towel on the rim of the lavatory, and came to greet her. As Vida stepped forward to meet him, the chiffon of the negligee pressed to her body, outlining her waist and the tiny cupped depression of her navel in the center of her stomach's slight swell. The flowing skirt was swept between her thighs as she moved, the shadow of her auburn pubic curls showing in their vee.

Foxx took her in his arms to kiss her. As their lips met and their bodies pressed together, he could feel the warmth of her skin pulsing through the thin chiffon, almost as soft as the skin it covered.

"I wish you were going with us," Vida whispered, rubbing her cheek on Foxx's naked shoulder as they broke the kiss. "It'd be awfully nice to have all that time together."

"We'll take a trip just by ourselves after we get back to San Francisco and things settle down," he promised.

"That's what we're always planning to do, but we never seem to be able to," she said. "Every time we get ready to slip away somewhere, you get a case that takes you out on the line. I'm getting a little bit jealous of the C&K Railroad, Foxx."

"If it hadn't been for the C&K, you and me might not've met each other," Foxx reminded her.

"Somehow, I think we would have." Vida smiled, turning her face up for him to kiss again.

Foxx felt the tip of her tongue slip out and run along his lips, and met it with the tip of his tongue. Vida's hand stroked the bare flesh of his side down to his hips and slid between their bodies to grasp the erection their first kiss had produced. Foxx released her from their embrace and cupped her breasts in his hands, gently rubbing his thumbs across their pouting, protruding tips.

A shudder of pleasure surged through Vida's body. Raising her free hand, she freed the clasp that held the neck of her negligee around her throat and shrugged her shoulders. The chiffon slid off her smooth white shoulders and rippled down to uncover her budded breasts.

Foxx bent to kiss them, and she responded by squeezing him harder with the hand that had been fondling his erection. By now Foxx was rigidly swollen. Vida began to rub her pubic brush with his tip.

Foxx put an arm around her and would have swung her onto the waiting bed but she shook her head.

"Not quite yet, Foxx," she whispered. "We don't have to hurry. Besides, the longer we wait, the more I'll want you, and the more I want you, the more pleasure you'll give me."

Foxx nodded and returned to kissing and caressing the firmed tips of her breasts with his lips and tongue. Vida's breathing quickened as his attentions continued. She let her negligee slip to the floor and turned her hips so that she could guide his throbbing erection between her thighs. She closed them, clasping Foxx firmly between warm pillars of firm but still yielding flesh. Squeezing her legs together, she began alternately tensing and relaxing the muscles of her thighs so that the heated flesh holding Foxx was first firm and pressing, then soft and yielding.

He stood quietly for a moment, then began to raise his hips and bring them forward when Vida relaxed her taut muscles. Her occasional deep inhalations broke the stateroom's silence more and more often, and after they'd swayed together in their rhythmic movements for a few moments longer, she pulled Foxx's head down to find his lips, and he opened them to her thrusting, questing tongue.

Vida broke the kiss to gasp, "The bed, now, Foxx! Hurry! I'm burning to have you inside me!"

In the small space of the stateroom the bed was not even a full step away. Foxx lifted Vida, his strong hands under her armpits, and bore her to the bed that waited behind her. They sank down, his body on her, and Vida found him with quick fingers and guided him into her. Foxx thrust hard into the moist warmth she'd opened for him, and held himself pressed hard against her.

With a strangled sigh Vida sprawled her legs to let him go deeper before she clasped her feet as high as she could around his waist and began rocking urgently. Foxx stroked in a slow even rhythm until her quick sighs and the frenzied writhings of her hips told him she was reaching an early spasm.

He drove harder and faster then, while Vida strained up to meet his deep, fast penetrations. Vida's sighs became low, throaty moans, then her body jerked and trembled and grew stiff. She held her soft hips hard against Foxx for a long shivering moment before she relaxed in a final trembling shudder. Her head fell back on the bed, her face smoothing to a contented smile in its frame of tousled red hair that fanned out on the white pillow.

"Oh, that was nice," she breathed after a moment. "It was so nice that I feel like going right on, if you do, too."

"Well, I ain't really stopped," Foxx said, smiling down at her. "So if you want to keep right on going along, I'm about as ready to as you are."

He had been holding himself pressed firmly against Vida while her spasm ran its course. Now he started to drive into her again, in slow deliberate lunges. For a long while she did not move to respond but seemed contented just to accept him.

Foxx did not hurry. He looked down at Vida's face, her eyes closed, her lips relaxed in a contented smile. Then he felt her inner muscles closing around him and saw her eyes open. Vida grasped her knees in her hands and pulled them apart, spreading her thighs wider and allowing Foxx to penetrate even deeper. Her body started to twitch and grow taut.

Still Foxx did not speed up the rhythm of his stroking. He waited until Vida's twitching grew into a steady heaving of her hips, until she wrapped her arms around his chest and buried her face in the taut curve between his neck and shoulder, holding herself almost suspended under him, her hips writhing and her buttocks coming up to meet him as he thrust down.

Foxx had felt himself building to a climax soon after Vida began to respond to his continued steady lunging. He held himself in control now as he started to speed his plunges, arching his back until he almost left Vida's body, then pounding hard when he thrust down into her hot, wet depths.

He moved even faster when Vida began to moan, and faster still as her moaning broke into quick sobbing gasps somewhere on the threshold between pain and unendurable pleasure. When at last he felt her trembling on the brink of orgasm, Foxx quickly built to join her.

Vida's body was soon tossing frantically, her hips twisting, her inner muscles grabbing at him. Foxx let himself go and began jetting, his hips thrust forward to pin Vida beneath him, and he held her there. She lay motionless except for the quick sharp contractions of the muscles that held him in her, while her arms dropped away and her head tossed, and her body relaxed as Foxx allowed his own muscles to relax and sprawled limply on her soft, hot flesh.

Bit by bit their strength flowed back. They shifted position slowly, moving and turning to find one in which they could be comfortable without breaking the bond of flesh which connected them.

They did not have to speak. Since their first meeting at the Petersen house some months ago, they'd been together often enough, either in the high bed in Vida's Pine Street flat or the wide, low bed in Foxx's Cosmopolitan Hotel suite in San Francisco for each one to sense the moves the other wanted to make. Lying at last on their sides, Foxx's lean hips still cradled between Vida's thighs, they faced one another, their heads resting on the same pillow.

"I hate to think of leaving tomorrow." Vida sighed. "This is the first chance we've had to be together since we left San Francisco. And from what Caleb says, it'll be three weeks or more before we get back from Mexico."

"Now, you know Caleb and Clara wouldn't hear of you staying behind, Vida, much as I'd like for you to."

"I'm not sure how much I'll enjoy traveling again," she said thoughtfully. "The two years my husband and I spent in Europe when we were first married gave me enough traveling to last forever, I think. If I hadn't needed to get out of the East when he died, I wouldn't have moved west. Not that I regret it, since it brought me out here to where you are."

"You'll enjoy it, once you start," Foxx told her. "Besides, soon as you leave tomorrow morning, I'm going out to the railhead, and that's where I'll be most of the time, I guess."

"If I stayed here, I could go out to the railhead with you," she suggested.

Foxx shook his head. "No. You never seen a railhead construction camp, Vida. It's not any place for a woman, except the kind that stays in Hell on Wheels."

"What on earth is Hell on Wheels?"

"Oh, that's what railroaders always call the shacktown that moves along with any railhead construction camp. I guess it got named that because some of the shacks stay on wheels to make it easy to move 'em to keep up with the camp. Mostly it's tents, though, for the whores and gamblers and saloons. A store or two, where the crew can buy things they need. But every Hell on Wheels is rough and mean, and I wouldn't want you in one of 'em."

"I'd feel safe anywhere, if you were with me, Foxx."

"That's the thing about it, Vida. Most of the time I'll be ranging out from the camp, looking for the place where them night riders is holed up. I wouldn't get to be with you any more'n we've been together coming down here from San Francisco."

"You will be careful, though, won't you, Foxx? I want you to be here when I get back."

"Oh, I'll look out for myself. You go on with Caleb and Clara, and enjoy looking at Mexico."

Vida sought Foxx's lips again. Her moist tongue tip crept between his lips, and as the kiss grew prolonged, Foxx began to swell once more. Vida pulled her head back and sighed happily.

"As long as I'm going to leave tomorrow," she said, "let's stop talking and make the most of tonight."

CHAPTER 3

"Well, it looks like you're ready to pull out," Foxx said to Caleb.

They were standing a few paces away from the carriage, a three-seat surrey, in which the party would travel to the steamboat landing on the Colorado. Caleb's clothing was a strange mixture. He had put aside the tall silk hat which he habitually wore in San Francisco in favor of a cream-colored Stetson creased in the flat-topped Arizona style. He had pulled on a linen travel duster, which gaped open to display his formal business suit, a long black coat and trousers, worn with a high-collared shirt and a dove-gray vest, and he was still wearing his citified patent-leather shoes.

Vida and Clara Petersen had also slipped dusters on over their traveling suits and had followed Caleb in switching to wide-brimmed Stetsons instead of their usual birdwing or fruit-ornamented summer straw hats. They were already in the surrey, occupying the middle seat. Tai Sun sat in the front seat beside the wagoner, and Magruder was in the back seat, which he and Caleb would share.

"I suppose so," Caleb said. "I'm still not really convinced that we need Magruder with us, but I can see that we might need him, even though I hope we don't."

"So can I," Foxx agreed. "I'd a damned sight rather see you have him and not need him than for you to need him and not have him."

"Yes, of course," Caleb replied hurriedly. He took an envelope from the breast pocket of his suit coat and handed it to Foxx. "I wrote this out last night. I know you won't use it unless you have to, but keep it just in case."

"What is it anyhow?" Foxx asked, turning the envelope over and finding it had been sealed.

"It's a letter that puts you in charge of all C&K operations in Sanders's section here, until we get back."

"Now, hold up a minute, Caleb!" Foxx protested. "I'm not a real railroader, like you and Sanders, or like your men in the main office in San Francisco! I've got all I want to do, being in charge of the detective force!"

"I understand that, Foxx. But I'm going to be out of touch with everything for the next three weeks, and I want you to be able to make any moves you need to in case there's trouble."

"Well—if you put it that way, I guess it's all right," Foxx said slowly. "But I sure hope I don't need to use it."

"So do I, Foxx." Caleb nodded. "So do I. Now, I'd better get in the surrey, or we're going to miss that steamboat."

Foxx waved good-bye to Vida and Clara as the wagoner geed up the team, and stood watching the surrey as it rolled past the roundhouse and division shops and took the old construction road along the right of way until it reached the river and turned south. Then he cut across the sidings to the one-room shack in the center of the yard which was Wade Benton's headquarters.

Benton looked up from the work schedules that were stacked on his unpainted wooden table and asked, "Well, Mr. Foxx, did you see the brass on his way?"

Foxx nodded. "Caleb and the ladies just pulled out."

"Is it all right for me to have the car shunted over to the shops so the windows can be fixed, then?"

"Let that wait until tomorrow, Benton, if you don't mind. I might want to sleep there again tonight, and I don't imagine I'd find a place in town that's as handy, or as comfortable."

"Whatever you say."

"I didn't stop in to talk to you about the car, though. I'm looking to give someone a little work. Know anyone who might be interested?"

Benton smiled. "Railroading draws all kinds. This man you're looking for, what would he have to do?"

"He might not have to do much of anything, but he might find hisself in a lot of sudden trouble. I'm not aiming to make a flunky out of him or give him much to do. He'd just sorta tag along with me, the way I was going to have Magruder do, and be around if I needed an extra set of hands to back me up in a tight spot."

"I get the idea you're going out looking for that bunch of night riders that shot up Mr. Petersen's car. Am I right?"

"You sure as hell are, but not just because they put a few bullets through Caleb's car. My hunch is they're the same outfit that killed the two men from my detective force."

"And that's what you want this man you're looking for to help you do?" Benton asked.

"Well, it'd be a real help if I can take along a man that's got some idea of how the land lays hereabouts. Oh, I've got my maps to go by, but there's a lot of things that maps don't show."

Benton rubbed his chin thoughtfully for a moment, then said, "There's one I can think of who just might do you, Mr. Foxx. His name's Pepper, but everybody calls him Tex, which I guess means he comes from Texas. I don't know anything about him except what I've noticed him doing on the job, but he's tough as a boot and ready to turn a hand to just about anything."

"How old of a man is he?"..

"Well, Tex won't ever be called a spring chicken again, but he gets around as spry as one. I'd put him at a little bit over forty. It's kind of hard to tell about a man like him. However old he is, it sure don't slow down his work."

Foxx grinned to take the sting out of his question before asking the yardmaster, "Now, I'll ask you a straight question and look for a straight answer. Suppose you tell me what's wrong with him. Why're you so ready to get rid of him, if he's as good a worker as you say he is?"

"Because he's hard to get along with, and he drinks too damn much," Benton replied unhesitatingly. "I've had to stop a few fights he's gotten into with some of the men in the gangs he was working with, and he's got two Rule G black marks against him."

"When you give him them two Rule G marks, how drunk was he?" Foxx asked.

"Well," Benton replied hesitantly, "he wasn't all that bad off, but you could smell him a mile away, like he'd just had a bath in the stuff. And he was talking a mite too loud."

"What kind of drunk does he turn into? Mean? Loud? And how drunk does he get when he goes over the line?"

Benton's brow wrinkled as he thought over Foxx's fast-fired questions. Finally he said carefully, "Why, I never have seen Tex falling-down drunk, or even staggering. I won't let the best man I've got break Rule G, though. If I do, I'm sticking my own neck out right alongside of his, and you know that's the truth, Mr. Foxx."

"Sure I do. What's this Pepper on the pay sheet for?"

"I just made him a gang-pusher, so he's drawing a full dollar a day now."

Foxx nodded. "I'd like to take a look at him. What part of the yard's his gang working in right now?"

"You won't see him or his gang around today," Benton said. "It's this month's swing day, so the crews that were on last night are working right through, and the old day crews won't show up until it's time to relieve them. But you can catch Pepper on the job tonight."

"Got any idea where I might run into him today, just sort of accidental-like?"

"Well, most of my men do their drinking at the Gold Spike Saloon. You can't miss it—there's not that many saloons in La Paz. I'd imagine you'll find him there, maybe not this early, but later on, in the afternoon."

"What's he look like?"

"Oh, he's sorta sawed-off. Pale-blue eyes and a weathery face with a big smashed-in nose and a little brush of a mustache that shows more gray than brown. Likely he'll need a shave."

"Thanks, Benton. I'll take a look at Pepper. And you might be thinking about anybody else you'd recommend, in case I don't like his style."

Until he stepped out of the yardmaster's shack, Foxx had been working on the momentum the night's fast-unfolding sequence of events had created. Now that he was faced with several hours of idleness, the momentum faded away, and the inevitable letdown set in. He found himself yawning and heavy-eyed as he stood, temporarily at loose ends, in the bright morning sunshine.

Lighting a stogie, Foxx retraced his steps across the yard to the private car. He hung his coat on a wall hook, unbuckled his pistol belt and hung it over the coat, levered his feet out of his water-buffalo hide field boots, and stretched out on his bed. Vida's perfume still clung to the covers and the pillows. With a smile of pleasure on his face Foxx dropped off to sleep.

In the middle of the afternoon Foxx's stomach woke him with a reminder that it needed to be filled. He splashed water on his face and swallowed a healthy eye-opener of Cyrus Noble, then foraged in the galley, making a meal of the baked ham and rolls left from last night's supper. He belted on his S&W, slipped his arms into his coat, and walked across the yards, past the depot. Stopping to light a curly stogie, he stood looking at the town that lay across the wide road beaten by the wagons hauling equipment when the rails were being laid. To someone like Foxx, who'd seen so many towns grow up beside railroad tracks, La Paz showed very clearly what it had been and what it was now.

To the west, near the riverbank, a straggling cluster of small weathered houses huddled. There was a sameness about the houses; all of them hugged the ground and looked as though they had grown up from seeds planted in the dry yellow soil. All of the houses were built from crudely squared slabs of the thin sandstone, ranging in hue from a faded pinkish brown to cream, that abounded in the region.

Stacked like bricks, the inch-thick slabs were laid in horizontal courses, the cracks chinked with mud from the riverbed. In such a rainless land mortar was unnecessary. With a few exceptions the houses had low-pitched tin roofs, most of them now brown with rust. If any of the wooden window frames or doors had been painted, no signs of paint remained. About half the houses were enclosed by fences made of branches thrust into the ground and woven together with wire. Gates were almost universally held up by twisted loops of wire instead of hinges, and almost universally the gates sagged mournfully.

Chickens scratched lazily in most of the fenced yards, and beside some of the dwellings goats or cows were tethered. This part of La Paz looked as though it had been standing unchanged for a hundred years, as perhaps it had.

Separated from the older houses by two hundred yards and a century of time, the new La Paz stood. To Foxx's knowledgeable eye it obviously owed its origin to the railroad. Many of the buildings which its businesses occupied had been left behind when Hell on Wheels moved east to follow the railhead and its free-spending construction workers, and beyond the business quarter there were still some of the tents which had been pitched when La Paz was the end of the line.

Among the tents a few small frame houses had been built. Only a few of these had been painted. Most of them glowed with the bright yellow of new lumber, and fresh lumber as well as glistening fresh paint also showed here and there along the street which faced the C&K tracks, where new stores or other businesses had moved in. There was a good mixture of older higgledy-piggledy structures among them, on which the paint had faded to a chalky drab or was peeling off in scabrous patches.

Except for the singularity of construction displayed by its original dwellings, La Paz, Arizona Territory, was a virtual twin to a dozen or more towns along the C&K's main routes that Foxx had seen altering from their original form and beginning to take on a fresh look due to the infusion of new life brought by the railroad's arrival. He scanned the signs above the street's business establishments: general store, hotel, café, doctor's office, barbershop, saloons, to the livery stable that stood at the end of the street. Foxx located the Gold Spike and angled across the broad, rutted roadway to its swinging doors.

Close up, the saloon showed the marks of an old building beneath its fresh paint. The latest coat did not quite hide the patches where older paint had blistered and peeled, or the gouges that a building's outside walls receive when it is skidded or hauled from one site to another. Foxx pushed through the batwings and stood for a moment looking over the establishment, letting his eyes adjust from the blazing sunshine to the dimness of the interior.

A long bar, freshly varnished, stretched from just inside the doorway to the back of the building. Only a handful of customers stood along the bar, and behind it there was a single barkeep, wearing the traditional white apron, which dropped from the middle of his chest to his knees. A dozen tables crammed the space between the bar and the side wall, but most of the space was taken up by a big rectangular table with a faro layout that stood against the wall. Three of the smaller tables were occupied by drinkers, and at one a five-handed poker game was in progress.

While he looked over the interior of the Gold Spike, Foxx also took note of the patrons. He saw no one fitting the sketchy description Benton had given him of Tex Pepper, so he sauntered casually down the bar almost to its end before stopping and resting a foot on the brass rail. The barkeep moved down to serve him. Foxx had already scanned the array of bottles on the backbar's shelves and spotted the one he'd hoped to find.

"I see you got a bottle of Cyrus Noble handy," he told the barkeep. He dug into his pocket and laid a half eagle on the bar. "A swallow of it'd go down pretty good right now."

Wordlessly the barkeep set the bottle of Noble and a glass in front of Foxx, filled the glass, and left the bottle standing within easy reach. The barkeep studied Foxx with a quick stock-taking look, and shoved the gold piece back across the bar.

"Just keep in mind how much you pour and settle up when you've finished," he told Foxx and went to serve a customer who'd just entered.

Foxx picked up the glass and swung around to rest his elbows on the bar while he faced the main area of the saloon. Sipping the Cyrus Noble in leisurely fashion, Foxx emptied the glass and refilled it before his inspection of the Gold Spike's patrons was completed.

Judging by their rough work clothing and grimy hands, he placed all but three of the eight or ten men as workers in the C&K yards or shops or roundhouse. Foxx switched his eyes to the poker table. He could not have failed to recognize the derby hat, checked suit, and pink shirt that tabbed a pink-cheeked man as a professional gambler.

Three of the others were C&K men, judging by their dress; the fifth had the swarthy complexion which spoke of Mexican or Indian blood. By the breadth of his cheek bones, the square line of his jaw, and his jet-black eyes with a vaguely Mongoloid slant,

Foxx decided he was part Indian. He was dressed in the brown duck jeans and checkered shirt of a cowhand.

Foxx had finished two jiggers of Noble and was working on a third before a man who filled Tex Pepper's description pushed through the swinging doors. He was slight of build, short, wore a mustache, and needed a shave. He had on baggy denim pants and a loose jacket of the material that most railroad yard workers favored. His hat set him apart from the other railroad laborers; most of them wore narrow-brimmed felts or derbies, while the newcomer's hat was a battered wide-brimmed Stetson with a Texas-style center crease and side dimples.

He walked with a self-confidence that just missed being a swagger as he passed by the patrons close to the door and stopped before reaching the spot where Foxx was standing. The barkeep was waiting with an unlabeled bottle from the backbar. He poured a drink and left the bottle standing on the bar in front of the newcomer.

Foxx moved down the bar and stood next to the new arrival, but before he could introduce himself, another new customer came through the swinging doors and inserted himself in the space between Foxx and the small man. The newest arrival was a Mexican wearing a charro outfit, a waist-length embroidered jacket and flare-legged trousers. He was a tall, lean man with a thin, straight nose, a lantern jaw, thick black eyebrows, and a sweeping tip-curled mustache; he might have been a ranch hand or a horse wrangler, Foxx thought.

Foxx waited until the Mexican was served before

moving around him. The small man had tossed off the shot of whiskey in a single gulp and was rolling a cornhusk cigarette.

Foxx said, "Your name'd be Tex Pepper, I guess."

Neither admitting nor denying his identity, the man studied Foxx's face with slitted blue eyes for a moment, then asked, "Do I know you from someplace?"

"We ain't been introduced, if that's what you mean," Foxx replied. "Name's Foxx. I work for the C&K, same as you do. Am I right about your name?"

"It's Pepper. But I ain't seen you around the yards."

"You wouldn't've. I work out of the main office in San Francisco, head of the C&K's detective division. Wade Benton told me I'd be likely to run into you here at the Gold Spike."

"Hell, you must've come in on that fancy private car, with the big boss hisself!"

"That's right." Foxx nodded.

"I don't recall doing anything a C&K fly cop'd be after me for," Pepper said. He drained his shot glass before adding, "And I don't imagine a high-up muckety-muck like you are would go out of his way to say hello to somebody like me just to be friendly. What's on your mind, Foxx?"

"It'll take a little bit of explaining, and I talk better when I'm comfortable," Foxx replied. "Suppose you leave your bottle and drink out of mine, and we'll go over to one of them tables and sit down."

"That's an invite I never can turn down." Pepper grinned. "Just lead the way."

Pepper left his bottle on the bar and followed Foxx

to a table just past the one at which the poker game was in progress. They squeezed between the closely spaced chairs, and the players looked up to see who was disturbing their game, then went back to playing as Foxx and his companion settled down at the adjoining table with their backs to the gamblers.

Foxx motioned to the bottle of Cyrus Noble and lighted a fresh stogie while he waited for the little man to refill his glass. Pepper sniffed the smoke that drifted his way and shook his head.

"That's some hell of a cigar you're smoking," he said. "What's it got in it? Bullshit?"

"I been afraid to try to find out," Foxx replied levelly. "Out in San Francisco the Italian fishermen smoke these curly little stogies, and I've just come to like 'em. They might have whale shit in 'em, for all I know."

Pepper grinned, twisting his short, brushy salt-and-pepper mustache. He pulled out a package of tobacco and a sheaf of trimmed cornhusks and started making a cigarette. "I don't suppose it could be much worse'n this Bull Durham I use. Now, I'm still waiting to hear why you was asking my boss about me."

"I wasn't asking about you in particular. He come up with your name when I told him I was looking for a good man to give me a hand on this job I'm here on."

"You said you was in charge of the C&K detectives?" Pepper waited for Foxx's nod, then asked, "You'd be looking for somebody that's robbed the road, something like that?"

"Something like that," Foxx agreed.

"How come you didn't bring somebody with you?

Didn't know you'd need help until after you got here?"

Instead of answering directly, Foxx said, "I guess you heard that Mr. Petersen's private car got shot up last night."

"It'd of been hard not to hear about it, the way things get talked around in a little bitty place like this."

Foxx explained, "I brought a man with me to take the place of that last C&K detective that got killed awhile back. After last night I figured I better send him along with Mr. Petersen and the ladies that're traveling with him."

"Which puts you a man short." Pepper nodded.

Before Foxx could reply, the Mexican who'd been drinking at the bar disturbed them by pushing along the backs of their chairs as he leaned over to say something to his countryman at the poker table. Absorbed in their conversation, neither Foxx or Pepper had noticed him leave the bar and approach; now Foxx shifted his chair to give the man room.

His movement disturbed the Mexican, who whirled when he felt the chair's back pressing on him. The glass of whiskey in his hand flew up, and the liquor splashed out, slopping over the gold-embroidered front of his charro jacket.

"¡Qué chapucería!" the Mexican snarled. "You are espeel my dreenk, *perro de Yanqui!*"

"Well, now, I'm right sorry about that," Foxx said. "But if you hadn't've shoved my chair around like you did—"

"¡Cállate, cabrón y hijo de cabrón!" the man broke in angrily. "¡Mira! Mi chaqueta, you are ruin! You weel buy me a new one! *¡Veinte dólares, dame pronto!*"

Pepper broke in to tell Foxx, "If you don't savvy his 'lingo, he says you got to give him twenty bucks for a new coat."

"Like hell, I will!" Foxx snorted. "It was his fault, not mine, him shoving my chair like he did."

"*¡No arguménteme, chingado gringo!*" the Mexican snapped, extending his hand. "*¡Dame el dinero!*"

Foxx shook his head. "I ain't about to give you a penny. It wasn't my fault you spilled your drink. If you think—"

Foxx saw the warning flicker in the Mexican's obsidian eyes as the man's outstretched hand began sweeping back to the pistol holstered on his hip, and that flicker was all the warning he needed.

Foxx dropped his hand to the butt of his Smith & Wesson in its cross-draw holster high on his left side. Before the Mexican could bring the muzzle of his revolver up, Foxx fired. The slug from the S&W pushed the charro-jacketed man into the poker table as the players scrambled to get out of the line of fire. The Mexican's shot, triggered by his dying reflex, thudded into the floor as the man slid slowly down the top of the upset table.

CHAPTER 4

In the silence that had settled over the saloon after the two shots, Foxx took a step away from the table to give himself room to move if necessary. The men at the bar were frozen in place; those who'd been in the poker game were still retreating from the overturned table.

Foxx broke the hush. "I guess enough of you seen what happened to know which one of us went for his gun first."

"If nobody else was looking, I sure was!" Pepper volunteered quickly. "This fellow in the cowhand's rig grabbed for his gun before Foxx did." He looked at the check-suited gambler, who was standing well away from the upset table. "You was watching, too, Ace. I seen you. Didn't that dead Mex start the fuss?"

"He did as near as I could tell." the man called Ace nodded. "It wasn't your friend started it. He didn't reach until after the Mexican started to draw."

"I'll count on you telling that to the sheriff, when he gets here," Foxx told the gambler.

"Oh, hell, Foxx!" Pepper snorted. "There ain't no sheriff in La Paz! The closest thing this burg's got to a lawman is the C&K's detectives, so you're the law, if anybody is."

"That's right," the barkeep seconded. He looked closely at Foxx, as though seeing him for the first time. "Is what Tex said right, friend? Are you one of the C&K's railroad policemen?"

"Name's Foxx. I'm chief of the C&K detective division," Foxx explained. "Out of the main office in San Francisco."

"Well, what Tex said is right, about the C&K police being all the law we've got here," the barkeep said. "So I guess it's up to you what to do. I don't know who that dead fellow is. He's been in a time or two before, but he never had much to say outside of ordering his drinks. I don't know where he lives or anything else."

Foxx looked at the Mexican who'd been sitting in the poker game. "He was coming to talk to you when all this ruckus got started," he said. "You know him, I guess?"

"*Si, señor.* Ees Raoul Morales," the man answered.

"He got a family? Or somebody he works for?"

For a moment the man seemed ready to reply, then his lips set in a firm line, and he shook his head. "I do not know thees, *señor.*"

"If you knowed him enough so's he'd come to talk to you, then I guess you know him well enough to take care of getting him put away," Foxx told the Mexican. "Am I right?"

With a shrug the man agreed. *"Creo que sí, señor.* I am know to find hees friends. Ees all right. I take care of heem."

"Can you haul him out of here right away?" the barkeep asked. When the Mexican nodded, the barkeep's eyes moved from one to another of the poker players before settling on one of them. He said, "Fred, if you'll give him a hand, your drinks are on the house the rest of the week."

His voice low, Foxx said to Pepper, "Looks to me like we better be getting out of here, now that's settled. I want to talk to you private, and there ain't going to be a way to do it as long as we're in here."

"Lead the way," Pepper answered. "I'll be right with you."

Foxx stepped around the two men who were picking up the dead man and stopped at the bar. He reached for his pocket, but the barkeep shook his head.

"I didn't know you was an important man with the railroad, Mr. Foxx," he said. "Drinks are on me, this time."

Foxx shook his head. "I'll pay." He took out the half eagle he'd offered before and put it on the bar. "Just chalk up whatever's left outa this to my credit. And do me a favor, if you will. See what you can find out about that fellow I had to shoot. I'll be in later to talk to you about him."

With Tex Pepper at his side Foxx pushed through the batwings and led the way across the yard to the private car. "This is the best place I can think of for us to talk in," he said, waving Pepper to one of the easy chairs. He lighted a stogie and sat down facing the small man. "Looks to me like the best place to start is where we left off. I've already told you why I need somebody to give me a hand on this case, and that Wade Benton put in a good word for you."

"Now, that was real nice of him, seeing I've rubbed old Wade the wrong way more times than one." Pepper grinned. "What sorta work you expect this man you're looking for to do, Foxx? I've done a lot of things in my life. Hell, I even rode with some cattleman's posses a few times, over Texas way, but I never tried my hand at detectiving before."

"I'll handle the detecting, Pepper. You'd sorta be riding shotgun."

"You tell me if I'm wrong, Foxx." Pepper frowned. He waved a hand to indicate the damaged interior of the private car. "But I'm guessing this job's got something to do with catching up them night riders that've been plaguing the C&K ever since you started pushing on east of here. Am I right?"

"Right on the nose. And I was just about to tell you I'm real sure it ain't just one or two men I'm going after. Chances are we'd be tangling with a pretty good-sized bunch. If you got anything against being shot at and shooting back, now's the time to tell me, so I can try to find somebody else."

"Oh, shit, Foxx! Any man worth his salt's been shot at more times than once by the time he gets as old as me!"

Foxx nodded. "It ain't all going to be shooting," he said. "Trailing, mostly, so if you can read signs, it'll come in handy. And I'd look for you to lend a hand with camp chores and jobs like that. I guess you know how to shoot a little bit?"

"Oh, I'm so-so with a pistol, not as good as I seen you are, back there in the Gold Spike." Pepper stopped and looked soberly at Foxx. "You don't think that fracas had anything to do with this case you're here on, do you?"

"It wouldn't surprise me," Foxx replied calmly. "I had the same idea the minute that Morales fellow got edgy so fast. A man's mostly got a reason to act like he did. But that's part of the job, too, Pepper. I'll leave it to you to say whether you want it or not."

Foxx had already made up his mind to hire Tex Pepper. He'd liked the way Pepper had stood his ground during the fracas in the Gold Spike, and the quickness of thought he'd shown while the gunsmoke of the shooting was still hanging in the air. Judging by the few men he'd seen at work on the C&K's La Paz division, he doubted that he'd find a man who'd suit him better. He puffed his stogie while he waited for Pepper's reply. It was not long in coming.

"I imagine this job'd pay a little bit better'n what I'm doing now, wouldn't it?"

"Some better. Back in San Francisco I start my new men at seventy-five dollars a month," Foxx said. "I don't see no reason why you ain't worth what they are, even if you ain't had as much experience as a man I'd generally be ready to hire."

"Well, now, Foxx"—Pepper smiled—"I don't expect you're apt to find many men in La Paz that's had a whole lot of experience at detectiving. Me, I don't claim to have none. But I won't argue about the pay. To tell you the truth, it's more'n I looked for it to be."

"You won't draw it long unless you're worth it," Foxx warned him. "And it ain't too easy of a job."

"It don't sound all that bad to me. I'll take you up, all right. When do I start?"

"Soon as I can get Wade Benton to let you off the job you got now," Foxx told Pepper. "He was nice enough to steer me to you, so I sure wouldn't want to put him in a bind and take one of his men away without giving him time to find a new one."

"That won't take but five minutes," Pepper said. "Wade's got two men on the extra board for every man working since construction at the railhead's slowed up so much."

"Just the same, I want to talk to him. Even if I know what he's going to say."

Pepper frowned. "What about a horse? I don't run to keeping one these days, nor saddle gear either."

"Neither do I, so we'll get fixed up at the livery stable. You might as well get your necessaries together and meet me there a little bit before daylight tomorrow."

"Getting my stuff ready won't take long," Pepper said. "All I got is my Colt and Winchester and bedroll and a change of clothes."

"All right," Foxx told him. "I'll go over now and have a word with Benton, then I'll see to getting some grub and saddle gear. You be at the livery on time tomorrow, because I'm set to pull out as soon as there's light enough to see by, and if you ain't ready, it won't hurt my feelings one bit if I have to go off without you."

* * *

Sunrise found Foxx and Pepper riding along the construction road beside the newly laid C&K rails that stretched through the crescent-shaped valley where the Bill Williams River flowed on its westward course. The rails ran in a string-straight line, but soon after they'd left La Paz, the Bill Williams swept south in a lazy, shallow arc before it recurved north to its juncture with the Santa Maria River. By midmorning the river itself was out of sight, and all they could see was the shelving northern wall of its wide valley on their left and a seemingly endless stretch of almost barren ground ahead and on their right.

Under the horses' hooves the surface of the construction road was rutted and dusty. The arid soil had been cut deeply by the wide iron tires of the big wagons that had hauled ties, ballast, rails, spikes, tie plates, fishplates, and bolts, as well as tools and supplies for the construction camp.

Under the bright sun, the windless day soon grew warm, and a fine powdery dust that the horses' hooves raised billowed up around them like a cloud. They began to sweat heavily, soaking quickly through the flannel shirts both men were wearing. Their sweat proved to be a magnet for the dust, which began caking on their shoulders and backs. Their perspiring faces attracted the dust as well, and soon they were forced to tie bandannas around their mouths and noses to shut out as much as possible of the acrid, stinging dust. The bandannas made breathing more pleasant but formed an effective barrier to their efforts to talk as they rode.

Twice during the long morning's ride they passed

places where the construction camp had stood for brief periods; the camp leapfrogged along the right-of-way, making jumps of eight or ten miles at each move, keeping near enough to the railhead to reduce the distance the wagons had to haul the materials needed by the work crews. At each place where the camp had stopped, Hell on Wheels had stopped, too, and the debris of its passage littered the areas where both camp and camp followers had stayed.

Debris and rails and the wide rutted road used by the wagons were the only signs of human habitation they encountered. Ahead of them the land stretched seemingly endless, a waste of yellow-brown soil broken by a few scattered clumps of gray-green sage and an occasional stand of stunted cedar trees only a little taller than the clusters of sage. In a few of the barren spots, as though they had purposely isolated themselves from other vegetation, a few lechuguille cactus grew.

In the clear morning air before the sun haze formed, they could see ahead the green-tipped brown slopes of the Hualapais. Impressive as the mountains were from a distance, both Foxx and Pepper were familiar with the illusions created by the clear air of the West. They knew it prevented a traveler unfamiliar with the terrain from making an accurate judgment of distance. Foxx had checked the route of the new line on the maps in the district superintendent's office and was well aware that the new line's railhead was more than sixty miles from La Paz and that the Hualapais were not as close as they seemed to be.

It was a land of desolation, much harsher than the great prairie, where Foxx had spent his Comanche boyhood. Although the territory itself was strange to Foxx, he'd seen so much similar desert country that he knew what to expect. He knew that the humps of the range would seem to stay the same distance away through the rest of the day and that the illusion would persist until the better part of another day had passed. By then they would have reached their destination, in the lower foothills of the Hualapais, a few miles north of the mouth of the Santa Maria River.

This was not country through which horses could be pushed. Foxx held their progress to a fast ground-eating walk, and as long as the river was near, detoured from the construction road at frequent intervals to let the animals drink from the light-greenish water. When the sun neared its zenith, the river was too far south to make a detour to its banks practical. Foxx began looking for a shady spot to stop and eat. As they pushed on and no shade came into view he pulled the bandanna down below his chin and turned to Pepper. He was surprised when his companion began laughing, great guffaws breaking the dusty crust which had formed on his bandanna.

"What in hell's so funny?" Foxx demanded. When Pepper pulled down his own bandanna to reply, Foxx saw the reason for the guffaws. Between Pepper's hatbrim and the line where the bandanna had rested, he looked like a man wearing a mask. Foxx chuckled, too.

"We look like the damned James boys, heading out to rob us a train, I guess," Pepper said, trying to wipe his face clean. "I never stopped to think that I'd look just like you when I pulled my bandanna off. What'd you start to say, anyhow?"

"I been looking for shade," Foxx replied. "I still don't see none up ahead, and it don't seem like there's about to be any for a spell. If you're hungry as I am, you won't object to setting under the horses' bellies while we eat a bite."

"Wouldn't be the first time I've had to make do with what was at hand," Pepper replied. "Pull up when you get ready."

"It might as well be here as anyplace else, then. Every place I look is just about the same."

They reined in and dropped the reins over the horses' heads; the liveryman had assured them that the animals had been broken to stand with dropped reins, and somewhat to Foxx's surprise they did. When the horses stopped moving, the dust stopped rising, though an occasional small puff spurted up under a scraped hoof. Under the horses' bellies and out of the now-beating sunshine, they sat and ate jerky and crackers, welcoming the tang of salt on the dry, thin crackers and washing down almost every bite of food with copious draughts of water.

After they'd taken the edge off their appetites and were eating more slowly, Pepper said thoughtfully, "You know, Foxx, I been thinking about the Mexican fellow you had to dust last night in the Gold Spike. Didn't something about him strike you as being sorta odd?"

"Two or three things hit me as being odd," Foxx replied. "Which one was you thinking about?"

"About how quick he was to pull down on you. Now, I seen more'n one gunfight start up, and unless there's been a quarrel or a fight between two men that gets into a shoot-out, things don't boil up all that fast."

"No, they don't," Foxx agreed. "And that fellow in the fancy rigging waited one hell of a long time to go over and pass the time of day with his friend at the poker table. When he first come in, he acted like he'd never seen that poker player before."

"You're figuring they was in cahoots?"

"It occurred to me after we'd left the place that they just might've been. That was after I got to thinking how that Morales fellow taken the long way around to get to the other one. He didn't have to push between my chair and that poker table."

"I hadn't thought about that, but you're right." Pepper frowned. "A thing like that sorta makes a man think the whole deal was rigged up beforehand."

"That come to my mind, too, but it don't make sense in one way. There wasn't no earthly way them two could've known beforehand that I'd go into that saloon."

"La Paz is a little bitty place," Pepper pointed out. "It don't take long for word to get around in a town like that."

"But I never heard of the Gold Spike until Wade Benton told me it was a sorta hangout for C&K people." Foxx stopped short and grunted in disgust. He said, "Looks like I ain't much of a detective, Pepper. If Wade knew the place was a C&K hangout, a lot of other people would, too. If somebody that knew the ropes around La Paz wanted to set up a play for me, they'd just naturally pick out the Gold Spike."

"Well, however slick them two planned their play,

it didn't do 'em no good," Pepper said. He brushed the cracker crumbs off his hands and began to roll a cornhusk cigarette.

Foxx took a stogie out of his pocket and touched a match to it. They sat smoking and thinking in silence for a while, then Foxx said, "We'd best go on. The day's wasting away fast, and there'll be plenty of time to talk when we stop tonight."

"Now, damn it, Foxx, I was just getting set to have me a nice siesta," Pepper said jokingly. "You know, the people who ain't got better sense than to live in this godforsaken country are smart enough to stay indoors in the middle of the day, when it's hotter'n the hinges on the devil's furnace."

"We'll put our siesta off until this evening. We still got a long ways to go, and we better make the most of every minute of daylight. Come on, let's get moving."

Through the rest of the afternoon they followed the same pattern that had served them during the early part of the day, pushing ahead slowly and steadily for an hour or so, then stopping to let the sweating horses rest for ten or fifteen minutes before moving on again.

Shortly before sunset the land began to slope upward ahead of them, and the right-of-way as well as the construction road ran through cuts made to level out the increasing grade. Though the altitude was not much greater, the rise began to show in the vegetation. The cedars were no longer quite as stunted, the sage grew thicker, and the gray-green blobs of the lacy lechuguillas disappeared entirely. Just before dark they reached a place where the construction camp had halted, and Foxx reined in when he saw the litter strewed across the landscape.

"This looks like a better place than most for us to stop in," he told Pepper. "I'd imagine we'll find a busted tie or two, maybe some old boards, that we can build a fire out of. If we stop now, we can scrounge around and get enough wood to build us a fire, so we'll have a good hot supper and coffee."

Foxx chose their campsite, a spot at the edge of the area where the construction camp had been located, beside a stand of cedars that would cut the cold night wind which he knew would blow up from the river soon after sunset. After tethering and unsaddling their horses, Foxx began rummaging in his saddlebags for cooking utensils and food. Pepper started for the old Hell on Wheels site where he had the best chance of picking up a few pieces of discarded boards. By the time Foxx had sliced bacon and potatoes and filled the coffeepot from his canteen, Pepper was back with an armful of burnable pieces of lumber.

"This oughta do us for supper and breakfast," he told Foxx as he dumped the load of boards and squatted down to start building a fire. "If it don't, there's plenty more where it come from. Whoever had one of them shanties over there must've had bad luck trying to move it. There's most of a floor left just waiting to be burned up."

"Well, we won't be here long enough to use more'n what you lugged in," Foxx said. He looked at the flickering fire, just lighted, and went on, "Now, I didn't have room to bring but one bottle of whiskey along, so we'll have to nurse it pretty stingy. I figure we can stand a drink before supper and another one afterwards, but that'll have to be the size of it."

"Two drinks is a hell of a sight better'n none at all," Pepper replied cheerfully. "I guess when you was talking about me to Wade, he mentioned that I like a good snort pretty regular."

"He said something to that effect," Foxx admitted, taking a shapeless bundle out of his saddlebags. He unwrapped the merino wool longjohns that had safeguarded the bottle of Cyrus Noble from the shocks it might suffer during a day's ride and popped the cork out.

"Well, I don't know what Wade said. You might have me figured for a bottle-buster. Which I ain't, Foxx. I take a drink when I feel like it, which is most of the time, I guess, but I don't suffer none without it."

"Just as long as you keep it that way, me and you will get along real fine, Tex," Foxx replied. He poured generously from the bottle into their tin cups. "In a job like this one there ain't no such thing as being off duty."

"I already figured that out." Pepper nodded. "Now, if you'll hand me the skillet, I'll put it on the fire, and while our grub's cooking, we can have a drink and a smoke."

Foxx and Pepper had already reached the stage, common to men of the western frontier, where they could get along without constant conversation. They finished their drinks and ate supper in companionable silence, downed their after-dinner coffee with a second swallow of bourbon, and silently sought their bedrolls.

Foxx lay awake for a while, smoking a last stogie, watching the small fire die to a glow of coals and listening to Pepper's snoring and the soft sighing of the rising night wind as it began to blow through the cedar trees that shielded their campsite. When the cigar had been reduced to a stub, he flipped it into the last of the embers, pulled his blankets up around his ears, and dropped off to sleep.

He did not know how long he'd been sleeping when the voice out of the darkness of the cedar grove reached his ears. He snapped awake at once when he heard his name called, and sat up, his hand going to the butt of the Smith & Wesson that lay at his side under the blankets. The last coals of the supper fire had died, and the darkness that surrounded him was velvet-black except for the faint sky glow the stars provided.

Foxx listened, but the silence was broken only by a soft shuffling of cloth from the spot where Pepper had spread his bedroll.

"Did you hear what I heard, Pepper, or was I dreaming?" Foxx asked in a low voice.

"I sure thought I heard something. Can't say what it was, though."

Almost before Pepper had stopped speaking, their doubts were removed when a man's voice sounded from the darkness of the cedar grove.

"Remain where you are, Foxx. And your friend, too. My men are all around you, and their rifles are ready. They will shoot without further orders if either of you tries to move."

CHAPTER 5

"Who in hell are you?" Foxx demanded.

"Who I am does not now matter," the unseen man replied. "I wish only to talk with you. Let that satisfy you!"

In spite of the warning the invisible visitor had given not to move, Foxx eased his S&W from beneath the blanket and held it ready. Either the unknown man had cat eyes or he heard the soft sounds Foxx had made, for his response was immediate.

"Do not try to use the gun you hold, Foxx!" he grated. "I have told you the truth about my men being ready with their rifles. One word from me, and they will kill you!"

"Not before I do a little shooting myself!" Foxx retorted. He was not yet sure whether he believed the threat. "You ain't going to get off scot-free if you start trouble!"

"I did not come to start trouble," the unseen man

replied. "And I have not come tonight as enemy. It is not needed that you worry for your lives if you obey my orders. I have told you, I wish nothing more than to talk."

Foxx was sure that the speaker's native language was Spanish rather than English. There was a softness in the cadence of his voice that was characteristic of Latin tongues, and his pattern of speech hinted that he'd rehearsed in his mind what he planned to say, only to have the Spanish placement of verbs and nouns creep into his sentences when he began concentrating on Foxx and Pepper.

To give himself time to think the situation through, Foxx stalled by saying, "I ain't used to talking to somebody I can't see. If you want to have a little visit, I'll get up and build a fresh fire, and we'll talk looking at each other."

"No!" The man's voice hardened angrily. "It shall be as I say, Foxx, not you!"

In a half-whisper Pepper said from his bedroll, "He might just be running a bluff, Foxx. Say the word and we'll call him."

"I do not advise you to try," the unseen man said quickly. Then, in a louder voice, he called, "*¡Chato! ¡Eusebio! ¡Guevavi! ¡Augusto! ¡Digan sus nombres, muestrenle que están aquí!*"

From the different points in the darkness that surrounded the camp, Foxx heard the men called by their leader repeat their names in response to the command. The names and the leader's use of Spanish reinforced his first suspicion that the band was predominantly Mexican, though he recognized two of the four names the leader had called as being Apache.

"You see now that I am not the bluff running, as your friend thinks," the night visitor said in the silence that fell after the last man had called out. He added, "I do not waste my time talking to this man with you. Tell him to be silent! I do not wish to kill him, but if he speaks again, he dies!"

"You heard what he said, Pepper," Foxx told his companion. "Just keep quiet, now, and let me and the man talk."

"You are sensible, Foxx," the unseen visitor said. "Now let us speak of the business we wish to do with you."

"All right," Foxx said, keeping his voice from giving away the angry frustration that had been building in him since the man had wakened him. "What'd you come to talk about?"

"You are a man of importance to the railroad, Foxx," was the reply. "There is a small favor I have come to request that you do for us."

"Who is this 'us' you're talking about?"

"If we can complete in a satisfactory manner the business I have come to discuss, you may find out later," the man replied. His voice was no longer harsh with anger.

"If you ain't going to tell me who you are, I ain't going to be inclined to listen to you," Foxx warned.

"You will listen because you have no choice but to do so! Think of the rifles aimed at you and your friend!"

"Well, I guess you got a point there," Foxx conceded. "All right. You better clear up whether you want to do business or get me to do you a favor, though. First you said a favor, now you're talking like you got a business deal. From what you said a minute ago, I'd guess it's got something to do with the C&K."

"You guess very well, Foxx. Whether you choose to call it a favor or a business matter is not important. If you do what we ask you to, I promise that you will be well paid."

"If you're going to pay me a lot of money, I wouldn't be doing you no favor," Foxx said quickly. "I'd be letting you bribe me, and that ain't my style at all."

"Does it matter what name you put on our payment, if it is large enough?"

"Maybe it don't make no difference to you, but it sure does to me. I ain't selling myself out for no amount of money."

"Perhaps you will change your mind when you hear what we wish to do and when I tell you how generous we will be."

"Like you said a minute ago, it don't seem like I got much choice but to listen, as long as your men got us covered. You'd go on talking whatever I say, so go ahead."

For a moment the night visitor remained silent, as though he was organizing his words. Then he said, "To carry the tracks of your railroad, you have men building a bridge across the Santa Maria River, yes?"

"So I been told. I ain't seen it, myself."

"But you know such a bridge is being built," the other insisted.

"Sure. It ain't much of a secret that railroads has to have bridges to go across rivers."

"It is not to our liking that this bridge be built, Foxx."

"I'd sure like to know who this 'we' is you keep talking about," Foxx said.

"I have told you that is not important. Now, about this bridge—"

"Hold on," Foxx interrupted. "If you'll listen to me a minute, I might just save you a lot of time. If you're fixing to tell me you'll pay me for stopping work on that bridge, you're talking to the wrong man. Even if I wanted to, I couldn't stop the C&K from building that bridge."

"Hah!" The sound was a snort of disbelief, not a laugh. "You say this only to deceive me, or perhaps to get a better price! Do not try to do such things, Foxx. We know how important you are in the railroad's affairs. We know you came here with the president of the railroad, traveling in his private coach. Ordinary men do not travel in such company and in such a fashion."

"I was in that private car because it was the fastest way to get me here. It sure wasn't because I got anything to say about running the C&K Railroad."

"You will stop lying to me!" This time there was both anger and menace in the speaker's tones. "We are not children playing games! We know too much for you to deceive us. Be honest with me, now. Tell me how much money you would expect to stop your men from working on this bridge."

"I been trying to tell you from the first, you're talking to the wrong man!" Foxx said, putting into his words as much conviction as he knew how to muster. "The only man on the C&K who can do that is the president of the railroad, the man I came out here with. But he'd tell you just the same thing, that he ain't interested in a proposition like that."

"It was our plan to talk to him," the voice said out of the blackness, "but he had gone before we could arrange to speak to him."

"Wait a minute," Foxx said quickly. "It was you and your bunch that shot up the C&K yards the other night, wasn't it?"

"I admit to nothing," the unseen man replied, but the smug satisfaction in his voice was as good as a confession. He went on, "But the president of your railroad must have learned that even the most powerful among you have no safety when determined men are willing to take risks."

"Hell, you wasn't taking no more risks the other night than you are right now!" Foxx said. "And you just wasted your time then, the same as you are now."

"Do not refuse our offer, Foxx!" the hidden speaker warned. "You and the railroad will both suffer great harm if work on the bridge over the Santa Maria River is not halted at once!"

"I guess that's a chance we'll just have to take, then."

"Think about my offer, Foxx," the unseen man urged. "Think about being a rich man! And for such a small effort. I will give you a short time to consider how great your gain will be. Within the next two days I will talk to you again and see if you have changed your mind."

"How do you know where I'll be in two days?" Foxx asked. "I might leave like Mr. Petersen did."

"We can find you, wherever you go."

"Don't bother. Take your favor or your business deal and go to hell! I ain't about to change my mind!"

"Almost you make me wish I had not promised that you will not be harmed tonight," the other said. "But I will prove to you that we keep our word. We will go now and leave you to think about what I have said. Do not move, Foxx, you or your companion. We go now, but you will not know when all my men have left, and you can be sure that as long as they stay watching you, they will kill you if you try to move from your beds."

"Now, wait a minute!" Foxx called. He stopped to give the night visitor a chance to reply but got no answer.

After a moment Pepper asked in a whisper, "You think they pulled out?"

"Hard to say." Foxx also kept his voice low. "I ain't heard nobody stirring, but that don't signify much. I got a hunch they might move out one at a time."

"You aiming for us to take after 'em?"

"Not for a minute, Pepper! We don't know but what there's one or two of 'em still out there, or how long they'll stay, if they are. Besides, we wouldn't have no more chance trailing 'em than a snowball in hell. They know the country, we don't. It's dark as pitch, all we'd be doing is thrashing around and wasting time. No, we'll see if we can pick up their tracks by daylight."

"That fellow who done the talking sure didn't make no bones about what he had in mind," Pepper observed.

"No. The son of a bitch leveled it out, whoever he was." Foxx sat up in his blankets and went on, "I'd guess we're all right now, as long as we stay in our bedrolls and don't try to get up for a while. And he didn't say we wasn't to move at all, just told us to stay where we are, so I aim to have me a smoke while we're figuring out what's the best way to handle this."

Foxx reached into his coat pocket and fished out a stogie. Closing his eyes to keep their pupils dilated while the match burned, he lighted the twisted cigar by feel. When he'd blown out the match, he opened his eyes again. The burning tip of the cigar seemed almost as bright as a lantern. It illuminated the area of the camp for his night-dilated eyes.

Pepper's blankets were moving, and a match flared as he lighted the cornhusk cigarette he'd rolled. Foxx got a quick glimpse of his grizzled face before the match was blown out. The glowing tips of the cigar and cigarette did their feeble best to break the night's blackness.

Foxx slid his hand into his vest pocket and touched the lever of his watch; the Pailliard repeater chimed twice, made an almost inaudible whirring sound, then tinkled twice again. Foxx grunted.

"What in hell kind of noise are you making over there?" Pepper asked curiously.

"Finding out what time of night it is. He sure picked a good time. Two thirty. Gives him and his outfit three hours in the dark to get away from us."

"You figure on taking after 'em when it's daylight, then?"

"Damned right, I am! I want to know where they come from. It can't be too far off. That Mexican kept talking about the Santa Maria River. I got a hunch we'll find they got a hidey-hole someplace along it."

"You've got the same idea I come up with, ain't you? That it's a bunch of Mexican bandits?"

"I ain't had much chance to figure anything at all yet, Pepper. The way that one that done the talking sounded, I pegged him for a Mexican right off. There was two Apaches in the bunch with him, though, going by the names we heard. I'd guess it's a mixed bunch, Mexican, Apache, maybe even a few Yaquis."

"This part of the Territory's full of all three," Pepper said. "And a lot of breeds, too."

"Stands to reason it would be," Foxx nodded. "Seeing as it belonged to the Apaches and Yaquis before the Mexicans taken it over, and then Old Rough and Ready got it for us back in '46." He stopped and scratched his chin thoughtfully, then asked, "Pepper, it just come to me that I didn't see more'n one or two Mexicans or breeds working at the C&K yards in La Paz. How come that?"

"As far as I know, damn few of 'em ever come looking for a job. There sure wasn't many on the construction gangs, either, when I was working the railhead for Pat Riley. Why?"

"Oh, no reason," Foxx evaded. "Just something that struck me, that's all."

Pepper said, "Well, hell, if we ain't going after that bunch until daylight, we might as well save our palaver. I feel like getting me a little bit more shut-eye while I got a chance to."

Foxx saw the glowing tip of his companion's cigarette disappear, and he heard the soft rubbing of shifted blankets. He was suddenly aware of the thin cold wind blowing from the south. Taking a last puff from his stogie, Foxx ground the coal out on the hard earth beside him, then lay down and pulled up his own blankets against the chill of the night. He put out of his mind the questions that were rolling through it and was soon asleep again.

Pepper was still sleeping soundly when Foxx woke. The false dawn was showing above the low, ragged line of the Aquarius Mountains, which lay east of the Hualapais and extended further to the south. Foxx sat up, pulled his blankets up around his shoulders, and lighted a stogie. His saddlebags were within reach; he brought out the bottle of Cyrus Noble and took a throat-warming swallow. He was just putting the bottle away when Pepper sat up.

"You ain't found it out yet, Foxx"—he grinned—"but there ain't a thing that'll wake me up quicker'n somebody pulling the cork out of a whiskey bottle. If it's that time of morning, I'll have a snort, too, thanks."

Foxx tossed him the bottle, and Pepper helped himself to a healthy swig before throwing it back.

"You get the fire going," Foxx told him, standing up to push his feet into his water-buffalo hide field boots. "I'll cut up some bacon for breakfast. We better eat something hot and filling now, because if we hit a good trail, we'll just grab a bite in the saddle at noon."

"Provided we hit any trail at all," Pepper replied. "The way that bunch sneaked up on us last night, I got me a hunch they might be right hard to track."

"All we can do is try," Foxx said. "It ain't going to make all that much difference if we get to the railhead today or tomorrow. It damn sure won't move very far between now and then."

By noon Foxx was almost in a mood to listen to Pepper's repeated suggestions that they were getting nowhere trying to track the men. When they'd first started following the gang, just before sunrise, the hoofprints of the five horses carrying the night visitors were faint but clear, even on hard-baked ground. The trail led them due south from the camp to a ford on the Bill Williams River, and the hoofprints showed clearly in the sand of the south bank of the river, where the party had emerged.

For the next three or four miles the riders had moved parallel to the stream, following its weaving course along the south bank. The hoofprints of their horses were clear, and Foxx and Pepper had no trouble following them until they reached another series of shallow riffles upstream from the place where they'd crossed first. Here the night riders had turned their horses and entered the water again. This time, though, there were no tracks on the north bank showing that the band had left the stream.

"They must've stayed in the river," Foxx told Pepper after they had ridden along the north bank for almost a mile in each direction, looking for hoofprints that would show where their quarry had come out on the bank. "We better split up here. You ride the south bank, and I'll take the north one. Sooner or later we'll find where they come out of the water."

They moved on upriver for another three or four miles, to a place where the water deepened into a series of huge pools, so deep that horses would be forced to swim in order to cross them. In the shallows downstream from the pools the river bottom was thickly covered with a layer of gummy clay, but the thick coating showed no signs of hoofprints.

After testing the consistency of the clay by riding across it twice, waiting for the water to clear, and then studying the hoofprints his horse had left, Foxx was positive the night riders had not come this far. The current at that point was too sluggish to scour the bottom quickly. He estimated that hoofprints pressed into the clay would stay visible for three or four days, possibly longer.

"Well, where do we go from here?" Pepper asked after they'd waded their mounts to the bank and lighted smokes. "They got to have come outa this river someplace, Foxx! I'm damned sure they didn't just turn into fish!"

Through the smoke of his stogie Foxx smiled thinly at the effort to make a joke. He said, "The best thing we can do is switch sides of the river and backtrack. You might see something I missed on the way, or I might see some sign you overlooked."

Foxx had not mentioned that he had been taught tracking during his Comanche youth by teachers who showed their students little patience and less mercy when the novices failed to follow a trail that their teachers had purposely made difficult, to test the youths to the utmost. Foxx was not yet sure of Pepper's tracking ability, but he had confidence in his own.

Pepper said, "Now, that's a good idee, Foxx! Four eyes is better'n two, like the eye doctor said when he told the old man he needed spectacles."

"Well, we'd better have our eyes fitted out, too, if we can't see a trail made by five men on horseback!"

"Down Texas way the Comanches and Kiowas used to ride half-wild nags that'd never been shod," Pepper frowned. "I've heard it said that when a horse ain't wearing shoes, it don't leave such good prints."

Foxx nodded. "The Comanches and Kiowas put big muffles made out of buffalo hide on their horses' hooves, too. That made it a lot harder to pick their tracks up. My hunch is that the Apaches with the bunch we're after used a trick like that to keep us from following 'em."

"How do we pick up their trail, then?"

"We just keep riding half-circles back and forth between where we are now and where we lost the tracks. Every time we finish a circle, we ride a bigger one. Muffles slows down a horse a lot, and sooner or later they'd stop and take 'em off."

"Why don't we save time, and start doing that now?" Pepper suggested.

"Because I want to look for myself along the way you rode when we come upstream," Foxx explained, then, to avoid hurting Pepper's feelings, added quickly, "And so you can look along the bank I was riding by. Anyhow, the only place we know to start from is downstream, where we lost the trail. And we'd better get started, because daylight won't last forever."

Foxx toed his horse's sides and urged it into the river. He kept his eyes in constant motion as he rode along the south bank, but when he'd reached the spot where the night riders had reentered the stream, he'd found no sign that they'd done anything except what their tracks seemed to show—vanished into thin air. He waved to Pepper to cross the stream and rejoin him.

"I thought we was going to do that circling thing you told me about," Pepper shouted.

"We are," Foxx called back. "But we'll start on this side. When that bunch left here, I'll bet a bottle of Noble to a glass of sarsaparilla they struck off south. Now, come on over here, and let's get started!"

"Looks like you'd be out a bottle of good whiskey if you'd made that bet you was talking about," Pepper told Foxx three hours later. "This is five circles we made, and we ain't seen nothing yet."

"And we might not for a while," Foxx replied. "Picking up a trail that's been covered good as this one has ain't something you do in an hour or two. It might take us two days to run across that trail, Pepper. But there's just one way to go about it, so let's keep on moving along."

They moved along, keeping a distance of a dozen feet between their horses, Pepper letting Foxx select the path, as they rode in one arc after another, expanding the perimeter of their course each time. They talked little; both men were concentrating on the stone-hard and generally barren ground, watching for a suspicious scuff mark, a freshly discarded cigarette or cigar butt, a heap of fresh horse manure, or signs of human excrement.

"Them fellows must've turned into ghosts," Pepper declared when they reined in at the riverbank after having made five more arcs. He looked at the surface of the Bill Williams River, reflecting in rippling flashes the rays of the low-hanging sun. "Damn it, Foxx, if they'd rode south like you figured they did, we'd sure have seen some sign of 'em by now."

"I got to admit it, Pepper," Foxx replied. "It looks like I made a bad call. I ain't saying I'm wrong yet, but we won't be able to do much more today. And I didn't bring an extra day's grub, which wasn't real smart."

"You mean we're going to have to sleep with empty bellies tonight?" Pepper asked.

"No. I mean we'd be fools to keep on looking today. The horses ain't in shape to take much more. They're worse off than we are." Foxx looked at the sun, low in the sky. "If we cut a straight line and move along steady, we oughta hit the railhead about an hour past sundown."

"That don't mean we're giving up, does it?"

"It sure as hell don't! We'll let the horses rest and eat good tomorrow, and the next day we'll start out fresh and pick up where we left off. Because this is the only lead we got to the men we're looking for."

CHAPTER 6

When Foxx announced his decision to push on to the construction camp, he and Pepper were still on the south bank of the Bill Williams River. They'd ended their last half-circle of searching just below the deep holes where the river bottom was so thickly coated with clay. Foxx took out his map and studied it.

"We'll be better off if we don't cross the river here," he told Pepper. "We got two tired horses on our hands right now, and this map shows four miles of right steep upslope between here and the C&K tracks. We'll miss the worst of the rise if we don't start north till we're a little ways further along. To save the horses, let's stay on this side of the river and ride east a spell before we cross and head north."

"I don't rightly mind which way we go, Foxx," Pepper said. "Just as long as we get to where there's something to eat before my belly starts yelling at me too loud. You sure you ain't got anything in them saddlebags we could chew on?"

"We finished off the bacon and spuds at breakfast," Foxx replied. "And that jerky and parched corn we put away at noon was all the other grub I brought along. I just plain didn't figure it'd be this long before we got to the railhead."

"Well, I've rode empty-belly before, and I guess I'll do it again," Pepper said philosophically. "So if you're ready, let's move on. Sooner we start, sooner we'll get some supper."

They headed east along the riverbank. Foxx rode close to the water's edge, dividing his attention between the terrain ahead and the river, looking for a place to ford the stream. The sun was off the water's surface by now, and through the slow crystal-clear current Foxx could see the bottom clearly.

After they passed the series of deep holes, the bottom began to shelve into narrow rock ledges, their jagged edges fringed with tiny tendrils of green moss that wavered through the clear shimmer of the flowing water. Foxx shook his head, knowing that a horse crossing a moss-bottomed river was always in danger of slipping. He kept looking for a graveled or sandy spot, where a shod hoof could get a secure footing.

For a full half-mile the rock-ledged bottom persisted, then the flat, layered stone began to give way to gravel. Looking ahead along the bank, Foxx saw that the gravel bed extended onto the shore. He was just turning to tell Pepper that they'd found a good spot to cross the stream when a dark blob at the edge of the light-ocher gravel bank caught his eye. They were still too far away for Foxx to be sure of what he thought he was seeing, but instead of starting across the stream he kept to the bank.

A few more minutes riding brought them close enough for Foxx to be sure the object was indeed what he'd hoped it was. He pointed to the brown mass and said to Pepper, "Look at that, Tex. I'd say we've just lucked out, whether we had a right to or not."

Pepper's eyes followed Foxx's pointing finger, and he let out a high-pitched Rebel yell. "Yee-ah-yah!" he shouted. "Fresh horse-shit! By God, we found what we been looking for, Foxx!"

"Sure seems like it," Foxx agreed. "It ain't likely anybody besides the bunch that visited us has come along here this morning." They reached the horse droppings, and Foxx dismounted. He leaned over the manure and prodded it with the toe of his boot. "It's fresh, all right. I'd say not a day old yet."

"Them bastards must've swum all the way through the deep spots, then," Pepper said.

"That's the only way they could've done it." Foxx nodded. "They'd've known this gravel bed was here, and figured they'd fool us." Then he added, "Which they did, until right now." He went back to his horse and swung into the saddle.

"You plan to try following whatever trail there is tonight?" Pepper asked.

Foxx shook his head. "It's too late, and we've got no grub. The horses are about wore out, too. No, we'll do what we set out to awhile ago, ride on to the construction camp and get some decent vittles and rest the horses a day. Now we know where to start looking, it won't be no trick at all to backtrack that bunch to wherever they got their hidey-hole."

They crossed the river and stopped on the north bank to let the horses drink while Foxx took a final look at his map and oriented himself by the setting sun to set a straight course to their destination. Keeping the sun at the correct angle over his left shoulder until it dropped below the horizon, he led the way through the waning daylight. The tired horses kept moving more and more slowly until they were barely plodding, their heads drooping, while night deepened around them. Foxx was ready to call a halt and let the animals rest when they mounted a long, low slope and he saw a faint glow in the sky ahead.

"We just about got it made," he told Pepper, pointing to the ghostly radiance that showed beyond a long, level plateau. "If we can hold out another half hour, and the horses don't give out, we'll be at the railhead sitting down to supper."

They slowly moved along until the glow sharpened into pinpoints of individual lights, and the buildings from which the lights shone became visible. Between Foxx and Pepper and the lights lay the construction camp. Foxx reined in when they got to its edge and studied the area, looking for the best way to cross.

Like all construction camps he'd ever visited or worked in, this one was made up of a few small wooden shacks and a half-dozen big tents. One of the tents served as a roundhouse, the cookshack and mess-hall occupied a second, and the others sheltered vulnerable or perishable supplies.

Track-laying materials covered the area around and between the tents and shacks. There were piles of ties, stacks of rails, boxes of fishplates and tie plates; barrels of spikes and crates of tools sprawled in orderly confusion over an acre of level ground. Beside the sidings stood the work engines and the high-roofed freight cars converted to bunkhouses for the crews and the outdated day coaches which had become the C&K's rolling railhead offices.

Most of the cars were dark, though lamplight glowed through the small square windows of several of the bunkhouse and office cars. Most of the light came from the buildings that stood in a long straggling line across the road from the construction camp, the community that followed the railheads of all the roads building major track extensions which railroad men universally had come to call Hell on Wheels.

This Hell on Wheels was small, Foxx thought, compared to a few he'd seen when the C&K was building its major mainline trackage. It was made up of some twenty or thirty buildings and tents of different sizes which stretched for more than a half-mile in a straggling, unevenly spaced line. In the lights that spilled through the open doorways of its buildings the silhouetted figures of men could be seen, trudging aimlessly as the off-duty work crews shifted from one of the settlement's distractions to another.

Dominating Hell on Wheels were the saloons. As though their proprietors had agreed to divide up the territory, they were spaced well apart, one near each end of the settlement, the third in its center. All three had high false fronts, rising well above the rooflines of the remaining buildings, and in the darkness the glow of lantern light through canvas revealed that the two largest saloons were tents behind the wooden fronts. The third and smallest was built of wood, and it had been constructed on heavy skid timbers which simplified moving it from one railhead stop to the next.

Outnumbering the saloons three to one were the whorehouses, with their red lanterns hanging over the doors. Some of the bordellos were tents, several were disguised as buildings by the same type of false wooden facades as the saloons, others were mere wooden shanties, and a few had been built on skid timbers. The houses were spaced along the street with no apparent agreement as to location. Four clustered together at one end of the settlement, the rest were scattered willy-nilly among the other commercial buildings.

There was a squat jerrybuilt structure which bore the single word "ROOMS" on its facade, another which looked more substantial had a sign announcing that it was the Arizona House. Two of the smaller buildings bore signs that read CAFÉ, and a red-and-white-striped pole in front of one small building marked it as a barbershop. A massive cutout of a molar proclaimed that Hell on Wheels boasted a dentist's office. One large tent had a canvas sign, GENERAL STORE, draped across its front. A modest-sized frame building bore the single word "MERCHANDISE" on the awning that shielded its door, and another was labeled DRY GOODS.

Apart from the other buildings at the east end of the line was the livery stable, which sported a huge wooden horseshoe on its front, and the remaining establishments either bore signs too small for Foxx to read from a distance or had no signs at all.

"I don't know about you, but I'm heading for one of them cafés before we look around for a place to sleep tonight," Pepper announced as they let the horses pick their way around the litter that surrounded the supply area.

"Oh, I'll be sitting right by you," Foxx said. "And I'll tell you this, when we set out the next time, there's going to be more grub in my saddlebags than there was when we rode out from La Paz."

"How long you figuring to stay here?" Pepper asked.

"We'll stay over tomorrow so the horses can get rested up," Foxx replied. "I need to have a talk with Pat Riley. And while we're resting, we can both do a little nosying around and see what kind of gossip we can pick up about what's been going on here. Next day'll be plenty of time to go back to the river and trail that bunch of night riders to wherever they come from."

"Let's eat before we start to worry about night riders," Pepper suggested. "Or about anything else. All I got in me now is air whistling from my guzzle to my bunghole."

They circled the railroad camp, left their horses at the livery stable, and joined the footloose crowd that was milling around in the long cleared space between the construction road and the limited attractions of Hell on Wheels. At the first café they came to, they went in and sat down.

"It won't make no difference which one we pick out," Foxx had told Pepper as they approached the settlement. "This time of night they'll all have beans and hash, and that'll be the size of it, so we might as well take the closest."

Foxx's prediction was half-correct. The café they came to first had hash but no beans. The hash was surprisingly tasty, but as Foxx pointed out after they'd cleaned their plates and were enjoying coffee and an after-dinner smoke, anything that tasted even a little bit like food would have been as good as a well-cooked steak.

"I'll save the steak for breakfast," Pepper said. "Right now, I'm in favor of sashaying on down to one of them saloons and having a drink or two."

"You go ahead," Foxx told him. "I better stop by the camp office and find out if Pat Riley's here or out at the railhead. If he ain't at the camp, we might not get to lay off tomorrow. I'll have to talk to him before we decide whether we can afford a day off."

"When you get through, you'll find me at whichever one of the saloons has got the best liquor and the prettiest dancing girls. Hell, I feel so good right now I might even dance with one or two of 'em."

"I can see that money you got when you was paid off at La Paz is burning a hole in your pocket." Foxx smiled. "Well, go on and spend it, Pepper. I won't have no trouble finding you after I've asked about Riley."

Somewhat to Foxx's surprise, he found Riley in the ancient day coach which had been converted into a combination office and living quarters for construction workers. Riley was a big man, both broad and long, with beefy hands and a wide, pugnacious jaw. He was what his ancestors long ago had dubbed "black Irish," with the swarthy complexion, ink-black eyes, and full, dark brows that had prompted the characterization. A rim of black hair shot lightly with gray showed below the brim of the derby hat he wore pushed back on his head.

"I'd offer you a drink, if it wasn't for Rule G," Riley told Foxx with a grin after they'd exchanged greetings.

"I'll take the will for the deed this time," Foxx said. "I guess I better follow Rule G, too, when I'm on the job."

"I've been halfway looking for you to show up," Riley said. "Really looked for you when that first man you sent out got killed, and when the next one was murdered so soon after he got here, I knew you'd show up pretty quick."

"I was gone, on a job up in Montana Territory," Foxx told the construction superintendent. "I got here fast as I could."

"Traveled in style, too, from what I heard." Riley grinned. "What brought the big brass himself out here? Is he just taking a vacation, or did he go down into Mexico on C&K business?"

Foxx avoided a direct reply. "You'd have to ask Caleb about that. He don't always tell me what he's doing, you know, even if he did give me a ride down here from San Francisco."

"I've been trying to neaten things up since I got word he'd be here," Riley said. "Hard to look good and keep my crews pushing iron at the same time. Especially with the trouble we've had the last six months."

"It's been going on that long?" Foxx frowned.

"Oh, maybe I stretched things a little bit, Foxx. Call it more like half that long. It just seems a lot longer to me."

"You got any idea of who's behind your troubles, Pat?"

Riley's broad Irish face grew dark with anger. "No, but I'd give a lot to get my hands on the murdering bastards! Oh, hell, Foxx, it could be anybody. You know, it wasn't until after the War'd been over a few years that the army had time to clean up the Territory. The place was full of Union deserters and Rebs that wouldn't surrender, and scalpers that were left from the old bounty-paying days."

"Wait a minute," Foxx broke in. "You mean there are still scalpers around here?"

"There are still a few. Renegades, mostly. It used to be that the Mexican government paid a bounty on Apache and Yaqui scalps. There was a lot of Indians killed for that bounty, Foxx. It's one reason why we've had so much trouble with the Apaches. They don't forget all that easy. They still blame all us whites for what the scalpers did in the old days."

"Is it the Indians that're slowing you down on laying trackage, then?" Foxx asked.

"I don't know for sure. Those men getting scalped gave me half an idea there's Indians mixed up in it somehow, that's all." Riley grinned ruefully. "I guess this job's the talk of the whole system, isn't it? Everybody saying Pat Riley's not pushing iron as fast as he ought to be?"

"Oh, I wouldn't say that, Pat. I just overheard some talk."

"Well, I might be able to push trackage a little bit

faster, but even if I did, it wouldn't do any good. We'd just have to stop and hold everything up when we got to the Santa Maria River. The crews are running behind on getting the bridge finished up there, and I can't just jump across the damn river."

"Any special reason why everything's slowed down so much?"

"Sure. And you'd understand why if you saw my pay sheets. These damn raids sure cut down on my work crews. I guess it's been four months since I've had all the steady men I need to keep the job moving."

"Four months ago was when the raids started?"

"About then. Railhead was back at La Paz when we had the first ones, and I'm not counting them. Then the damned night-riding bastards just followed us along when we begun pushing iron east. The last few times they haven't hit the camp here. They've raided the bridge crew up at the Santa Maria River."

"How many men have you lost, all told?" Foxx asked.

"That's hard to say."

"I don't see why it should be."

"Now, Foxx, you know the kind of men we get on construction crews," Riley said. "Drifters, a lot of 'em. They work here awhile, then move on to where the Santa Fe or SP or UP is pushing iron. Some of 'em don't even draw down their time, they just get itchy feet and start traveling. When I come up a man short, how in hell am I going to know if he's just moved on or if he's got himself killed by the night riders?"

"No," Foxx agreed thoughtfully, "I guess you can't always tell, unless you find his body."

"Well, we've only had four bodies show up, so far. Your two detectives were the latest. Before that, there were two more. One was a gandydancer and the other one was just a strong back, and you know as well as I do, Foxx, that both of 'em are a dime a dozen in a railhead camp."

"How come you didn't report it to San Francisco when them first two got killed, Pat?" Foxx asked.

"Why, hell's bells, I did report it! Not direct, of course. You know all my reports go to the division super, and he boils 'em down before sending 'em in to the main office." Riley stared at Foxx for a moment before asking, "You mean Frank didn't report anything about those first two killings?"

"That's what I asked Caleb, Pat. He said he hadn't heard a word about anybody getting killed until that first detective I sent out here was murdered."

"Well, Frank got every bit of what's been going on in my reports. I guess you'll have to ask him why."

"I will. Soon as he gets back to La Paz. But that's still to come." Foxx took out a stogie and lighted it before he said, "Tell me a little bit about that bridge job, Pat. Is there anything special about it?"

"As far as I'm concerned, it's just another bridge. Why?"

"I'm just wondering. When did you start work on it?"

"Let's see—three—no, four months ago. That was when I sent the first trestle timbers up in wagons."

"Did it ever occur to you that them raids started about the same time?" Foxx asked casually.

Riley's brow buckled into a frown. "I never thought of it, but you're right. It never did occur to me to connect the bridge and the raids."

"No reason why you should have. That's the kind of thing I'm supposed to think about." Foxx puffed his stogie to keep it from going out, then asked, "Have you asked the army to send a squad or two up here to guard your bridge crew, Pat?"

"Sure. More than once. Not that it's done any good. The big trouble is that there aren't all that many soldiers up here in the northern part of the Territory. Fort Whipple, up at the capital at Prescott, is the closest, but it's better than two hundred miles east of here. If you look in the other direction, Fort Mojave's even further off. We can't count on the army for help."

"All you've got for guard duty is Jim Flaherty's policemen, then? Four or five of them, as I recall."

"Four. I've got to have one of them here to keep things fairly quiet across the road, in Hell on Wheels. Of course, we lost a lot of tents when we moved out of La Paz. Some stayed there, and a few didn't make it all the way here. One man can handle what's left. Anyhow, that leaves three policemen to station at the bridge, and none at my railhead camp."

"I can't help you much either, not right away. I've got a man with me, not one of my regulars, just a fill-in. The man I brought from the main office to replace Hanson is keeping an eye on Caleb and Mrs. Petersen right now. But I'll send a wire to Flaherty and see if he can't move some of his uniformed men here right quick. I guess you've got rifles for the crews?"

"Ten. That was all the general storekeeper said he had on hand. He told me I didn't need any, said the Indians here in Arizona Territory are peaceful."

"Well, at least you've got a few guns at the bridge and railhead," Foxx said. "That's better'n not having any."

"Sure, but the way the night riders come in so fast and get away even faster, the guns haven't been much use, either at the railhead or at the river."

"How far is everyplace from everyplace else, Pat? I've got survey maps, but I ain't too sure how right they are."

"We're just over forty miles from La Paz right here. The railhead is fifteen miles east, the river's another ten. Damn it, Foxx, I had all this stuff in my reports when I asked Flaherty to send me a few more men. He never did even answer."

"Like I told you, Pat, I been up in Montana Territory, and I ain't kept track of things the way I would've if I'd been in San Francisco. It looks to me like there's a lot of loose ends here that need tying up. I'll see what I can do."

"You'll be here awhile, then?"

"Long enough to get things straightened out."

"I guess you'll want to go up to the railhead and then on to the bridge and take a look around?"

"I'll have to put that off a little while, Pat. There's a little job I want to take care of first. A lead I need to look into. Something that Pepper and me run into on the way up here."

"You're not talking about Tex Pepper, are you?"

"I sure am. You know him?"

"If he's—hell, there couldn't be two men with the

same name around here. Feisty little sawed-off fellow with a brushy mustache? Older than most of the men?"

"It's the same one. Why?"

"I remember him working on one of my crews. Had to give him back to Wade. Have you had any trouble keeping him sober?"

"Not so far. Of course, he ain't been in much of a place where he could get too much to drink. But I'll keep what you said in mind while we're around here. And pass the word on to that policeman of Flaherty's to call me if Pepper gives him a bad time, will you?"

"Glad to." Riley hesitated before asking Foxx, "I don't like to butt into another man's affairs, but is that lead you're looking into connected with the night riders?"

"I might have a line on 'em," Foxx replied noncommittally. He lighted a fresh stogie from the butt of the one he'd smoked down and went on, "Stands to reason they've got a hideout close by here. I don't guess you've sent anybody out trying to find it, have you?"

"Damn it, Foxx, I'm a construction man, not an Indian scout! This country's so cut up with ravines and box canyons and valleys where rivers used to run that a man who doesn't know too much about it could prowl around a year without finding anything!"

"I noticed that while me and Pepper was riding up here."

"Well, if I can help—"

"Thanks, Pat. I'll sing out if I need to."

"Will you want to stay in one of the bunkhouses

while you're here, Foxx? There's more than enough room."

"If it's all the same to you, I'll stop over across the road. I had my fill of bunkhouse cars quite awhile back. I noticed there's two rooming houses across the way. Which one is the best?"

"Get a room at the Arizona House, if you can. Old Bob House throws out the drunks and whores and goes over his mattresses with kerosene once a week."

"Thanks." Foxx stood up and stretched. "Well, I'm about due to turn in. Didn't get too much sleep last night. Me and Pepper won't be starting out until day after tomorrow, Pat, so I'll look in tomorrow and send some wires back to San Francisco."

"I'll be around," Riley promised.

Foxx left the office and stood outside in the cool night air for a few moments, thinking over what Pat Riley had told him. Then he consigned the problems to the back of his mind until tomorrow and started across the construction road to Hell on Wheels.

CHAPTER 7

Hell on Wheels showed signs that it was beginning to wind down for the night. Foxx stopped at the edge of the construction road and looked across at the settlement. The activity around the doors of the saloons and brothels had dropped sharply; it was not nearly as crowded as it was when he and Pepper had emerged from the café after supper.

Both of the restaurants were dark now, as were all but one of the merchandising establishments. Only the saloon and the livery stable were brightly lighted; the whorehouses kept their window curtains drawn and showed their inside lights only when a patron entered or left, but the red lanterns above their doors still glowed invitingly.

Since the big saloon that stood in the center of Hell on Wheels was almost directly in front of him, Foxx decided to look there for Pepper before walking to either end of the long street. He strolled across the road and the stretch of cleared ground that stood between the road and the buildings. Then he pushed through the batwings and stood for a moment just inside the door, surveying the cavernous interior.

Acetylene lamps hung from each of the two poles that supported the big tent hidden behind the saloon's false front. The bar was long, curved, and well-lined with customers; three barkeepers were stationed behind it, and they were in constant motion, filling and refilling glasses, whisking away used ones, and making change. Tables filled the area in front of the U-shaped bar, covering a bit more than half the floor. The other half was devoted to gambling.

In addition to a half-dozen round poker tables in the center of the gambling area, there were large rectangular keno tables along the canvas wall. The table in the center of this array had a metal chuck-a-luck funnel suspended above the dealer's cutout. Faro layouts were on the green felt tops of the two tables at the end of the line. The large tables were not in use, though; the lamps suspended from a rope rigging that ran above them were dark.

Play was going strong at most of the poker tables, and the click of chips and coins and the low voices of the gamblers provided a soft undertone to the laughter and loud talk from the bar. Between the section filled by the poker tables and the line of tables along the wall, two small square tables filled a small arc of space. Pepper was sitting at one of them, absorbed in a game of three-card monte.

Pepper had not seen Foxx come in. His eyes were fixed on the hands of the dealer, whom Foxx could not see because of the men at the poker tables between him and the monte game. Not wanting to disturb Pepper, Foxx headed for the bar. After he'd ordered and been served a drink of his favorite bourbon, he turned to look at the gambling area again. He could see Pepper's face clearly, but the crowded poker tables continued to block his vision. Foxx took a half step along the bar, and his jaw dropped when he saw that the monte dealer whose turns Pepper was bucking was a woman.

He could still see very little, though. The woman was facing away from the bar, and Foxx could get only an occasional glimpse of the top of her head. She wore her shining coal-black hair in thick twin plaits, brought up from the nape of her neck over the crown of her head in the fashion of a tiara. The plaits were adorned by a wide tortoiseshell comb. He could not tell whether the woman was young, old, or middle-aged, and his curiosity was mounting by the minute.

Finishing his drink, Foxx turned to put the empty glass on the bar; a barkeep was standing ready to refill it, the bottle of Cyrus Noble already tilted to pour. Foxx nodded, paid for the drink, and started circling around the perimeter of the saloon to get a clear look at the woman monte dealer. He finally reached a spot at the rear of the big barroom where he could see her face. The first thing that registered in his mind as he studied her was her youthfulness.

She appeared to be little more than a girl. Her glossy hair and thick eyebrows were midnight black; the hair and her dark eyes, high cheekbones, straight nose with flaring nostrils, and full, pouting lips showed her Hispanic ancestry. She wore a blouse, low-cut, with a deep half-moon neckline that dropped to the vee of her generous, full breasts; the spangles with which the blouse was embroidered caught the lamplight and shot out tiny flashes of red, blue, green, and yellow.

Both Pepper and the dealer were absorbed in the game. Two or three stacks of coins stood on the table in front of Pepper, and as Foxx watched, he took several coins off one of the stacks and put them at the bottom edge of one of the three cards that lay facedown on the table. The girl said something to him, and Pepper shook his head. She flipped over the card he'd chosen, touching it with only her fingertips. Pepper scowled and thudded his fist on the tabletop. The dealer shrugged and pulled the bet across the table to the scattered pile of coins in front of her.

Curiosity as much as a concern for Pepper's welfare prompted Foxx to take a hand in the proceedings. He made his way toward the table and was almost at Pepper's side before the small man saw him.

"Well, by God, Foxx!" he said. "I was just killing time waiting for you and figured I'd try my luck while I waited. This here's Lita. Besides her being about the prettiest monte dealer I ever run across, she really deals a mean hand, too."

Foxx touched his hat brim with a forefinger, and Lita replied to the salute with a smile and a nod. At close range he could see that the dealer was older than he'd thought. There were thin lines running from the edges of her nostrils to the corners of her pouting lips, and the beginning of a small double chin under the still-clean line of her rounded jaw hinted at her real age.

Foxx said to Pepper, "I got my business taken care of. Any time you're ready, we can go over and get us a place to sleep. Riley said to try the Arizona House."

"You go on, and I'll be along in a little while," Pepper said. He frowned. "I got to see if I can't get back what Lita's won from me. She's been moving them cards faster'n I can see ever since I set down here."

"Oh, I ain't in all that big of a hurry," Foxx replied. "I'll watch and see how you come out on the next hand or two."

"Set in with me," Pepper suggested. "Maybe it'll change my luck."

"No, thanks. I'll just watch," Foxx replied.

He hadn't expected the dealer to second Pepper's invitation. Three-card monte was a one-on-one game, a lone player against the dealer. The player risked his stakes on his ability to keep his eyes on the card he'd bet on, outwitting the flying fingers of the dealer as the three cards which gave the game its name were shuffled from one hand to the other. When other players joined in the game, the dealer was forced to work harder; to keep the house odds from being reduced, a separate layout and shuffle were required for each bettor.

"If you are ready, then, Pepper," Lita said; it was a question rather than a statement. There was only the slightest hint of an accent in her soft, well-modulated voice.

"Ready as I'll ever be. Go on, lay 'em out."

Scooping up the three cards from the old layout, Lita tossed them to one side of the table, atop a stack that already lay there. She picked up the deck, slid three cards off its top, and laid them face up on the table; they were the trey of spades, the ten of hearts, and the jack of clubs.

Pepper tapped the jack with a grimy fingertip. Lita picked up the three cards and began to strip-shuffle them, from one hand to the other, turning them to expose alternately their faces and their backs. Then she laid the three pasteboards in a neat row on the table, face down.

Pepper studied the backs of the cards for a moment, one hand toying with a stack of the money in front of him. He took a few coins from the stack and placed them at the bottom edge of the center card. Again using only her fingertips, Lita flipped the card faceup. It was the spade trey.

"You are not favored by the cards tonight," Lita observed.

"That's sure the truth," Pepper agreed.

Lita smiled sympathetically at Pepper as she turned the two remaining cards to show the jack on one side of the trey, the heart ten on the other side. She drew Pepper's money toward her, gathered the cards up, and added them to the discard pile.

"I guess I need a drink to change my luck," Pepper announced. He looked up at Foxx. "How about you keeping my chair warm while I go over to the bar?"

Foxx shrugged. "I don't imagine Lita cares much whether she wins your money or mine," he said, taking any sting out of his words with a smile at the dealer. "And I ain't bucked a monte layout for a long time. Go on, Pepper. I'll see if my luck's running any better'n yours has been."

Lita kept her eyes on Foxx, studying his face, while

he settled into the chair Pepper had vacated and took money from his pocket. Still without speaking she slid three fresh cards from the top of the deck and spread them face up, showing the queen of diamonds, the four of clubs, and the spade six.

"Maybe the lady'll bring me luck," Foxx said. He tapped the queen.

"Would your luck not depend on who the lady is?" Lita asked with a smile that showed her even white teeth.

"We'll just have to wait and see, won't we?"

Foxx watched Lita's quick-moving fingers as she shuffled the three cards, exposing their faces and backs in turn. She laid the cards facedown, and Foxx pushed a half eagle across the table to the edge of the card at the right end of the layout.

Lita turned the card. It was the queen.

"Your lady was indeed lucky for you," she said, stacking five cartwheels beside Foxx's gold piece. "Will you bet again?"

"Sure. As long as I'm playing with house money," he said, pulling the gold piece back and leaving his winnings as a stake for the next turn.

On the next deal Foxx won again, picking the eight of diamonds from the three-card layout. The deal had exhausted the deck, and Lita took an unopened one from a drawer in the table. She broke the seal, riffled through the cards, discarded the joker, and shuffled, her fingers twinkling expertly as she shuffled a half-dozen times.

Lita lifted off the three top cards and spread them out. Foxx saw that he had to choose between the trey of hearts, the ace of spades, and the king of clubs. Unhesitatingly he tapped the black ace.

"You must be a very brave man," Lita said as she began to strip-shuffle the three cards.

"What gives you that idea?"

"Because you have chosen to make your bet on the card of death."

"Maybe I just ain't superstitious," Foxx replied.

He lighted one of his twisted stogies while he watched Lita place the cards on the table face down, then he moved the stack of silver dollars across from the edge of the right-hand card to the one on the opposite end. Lita turned over the card; it was the spade ace Foxx had bet on.

"Your eye is quicker than my hand, I see," she commented.

Foxx smiled across the table at her and said, "Either that, or my luck's running a little bit ahead of yours."

Lita paid Foxx with another stack of coins, which she pushed up beside his stake. She picked up the deck, ready to deal again, but before she could begin dealing, Pepper returned from the bar, carrying his drink. Lita rested her hand on the table, the deck in her palm, while she waited for him to speak.

"You having any better luck than I did, Foxx?" Pepper asked.

"I ain't complaining," Foxx told him. "But I'm ready to give your chair back to you."

"Not even one more turn?" Lita asked Foxx quickly. "You have won from me three times. I should have one chance to get at least part of my money back."

She moved the hand holding the cards, not an obvious move, but one that seemed perfectly natural. Foxx glanced at the cards, and his quick eyes spotted the small blemish, a bent corner on the card on top of the deck. He said nothing, certain in his mind of what was going to follow.

"If you're running a lucky streak, don't bust it," Pepper said. "It won't hurt my feelings a bit if you win again."

Lita looked questioningly at Foxx. "Will you play, then?"

"Seeing as I'm still betting with house money," Foxx said, "I wouldn't lose a penny if I made a bad guess this time. And on account of it's going to be my last deal, I'll just let what's on the table ride."

Without looking at the deck, which she still held facedown in her hand, Lita turned up the three top cards. The first was the jack of diamonds, the second was the seven of clubs, the third was the diamond five.

Foxx tapped the jack, saying, "That bad-luck ace won for me, and I got a hunch this bad-luck jack might, too."

Lita put the deck on the table, picked up the three cards, and began shuffling them.

"Don't lose sight of that jack, now," Pepper cautioned him.

Foxx nodded. He was keeping his eyes on Lita's hands as she strip-shuffled, but her skill was great enough to hide the maneuver. She spread the three cards facedown on the table.

Foxx saw the blemished card at once, lying in the center. He moved his stake slowly as though he intended to place it at the bottom of the center card, but before he released the two stacks of coins, he moved them back to the edge of the card where they had originally rested.

"I had good luck with the end card last time," he said, watching Lita's face. "Let's see if it still holds."

Foxx saw the flicker of a frown pass over Lita's face, and he suppressed a chuckle. He'd seen enough three-card monte games to recognize the old professional's trick of showing a too-eager gambler the back of a card that could be readily identified because of a characteristic bend or a dog-eared corner, and then, while strip-shuffling, uncrimping the bent card and marking another card the same way. He admitted to himself, though, that Lita had performed the move with as much skill as any gambler he'd ever seen.

Lita's frown lasted such a brief fraction of a second that Foxx barely saw it, and he could tell that Pepper had missed it completely. The smile she'd displayed throughout their play returned to her lips as she turned over the cards. It widened when she saw the bland, frozen face of the diamond jack exposed.

"I am glad you had already decided to stop," she said, tossing the three cards in the discard pile. "Your luck is too good for me. I will be better off playing against your friend."

"Don't be so sure about that," Pepper said. "Maybe Foxx has changed the way the luck's running tonight."

Foxx stood up, dropping his winnings in his pocket. He said, "The least I can do is have the barkeep bring you a drink. And I owe you one, too, Pepper, for telling me I oughta play out that last deal. When Lita cleans you out, come on over to the Arizona House. I'm going right on to bed, but I'll pay for both of our rooms, so don't let 'em charge you for yours."

Pepper nodded absently. His attention was already on Lita's hands, which were picking up the deck.

Lita said, "You must come back soon, Foxx, when my luck has changed."

"A lady as pretty as you don't need luck," Foxx replied. "Me and Pepper's going to be around awhile, though, so I'll likely give you another chance at what little bankroll I got."

Stopping at the bar, Foxx had another drink for himself and paid for those he'd promised to send over to Pepper and Lita. He stepped outside into the night, found the air had cooled appreciably while he'd been in the saloon, and strolled slowly along the rough dirt strip that lay between Hell on Wheels's buildings and the construction road.

He reached the Arizona House and went inside. The small entryway also served as a lobby; a narrow table stood against one wall, and on it a kerosene lamp burned beside a battered ledger, an inkwell with a pen leaning in it, and a push bell. A hand-lettered sign propped against the lamp read RING FOR SERVICE.

Foxx rang. After a few moments a lanky man, collarless, his suspenders dangling down his back, appeared in the hallway. Rubbing his eyes as he moved, the man ambled leisurely up to Foxx and inspected him sleepily.

"Looking for a room, I guess?" he asked through a yawn.

"Two rooms," Foxx replied. "One for me and one for a man named Tex Pepper. He'll be along later on. I'll pay for both rooms now."

"C&K men, I suppose? If you are, your credit's good."

"You suppose right. Pat Riley told us to try here."

"Always got a room for you railroaders. Special half-price rate, too. Six bits a night for a regular dollar and a half room. Baths are a quarter, if you want one."

"Now, that's the best offer I've had tonight," Foxx said. "I could sure use a bath right now." He signed the register and put a gold eagle on the table. "Mark that up to my account. My friend and me'll be here a day or two. I'll settle for whatever else is due when we leave."

"That'll be fine, Mr.—" The man looked at Foxx's signature and scratched his head. "Foxx? Is that all the name you got?"

"It's all I need, ain't it?"

"Well, when you put it like that, I guess it is." The man took the pen and wrote a room number beside Foxx's name. "I'll put you downstairs here, room ten. Have to put your friend upstairs, though. No more rooms down here."

"He won't mind, and I won't either," Foxx said.

"Long as it don't matter, then." The clerk nodded. "Ten's next to the bathroom. Water in the pitcher's fresh. Privy's right out back. Room key's in the door. Hand it in when you check out. Anything else?"

"Seems to me like you've covered things pretty thorough."

"Bid you good night, then," the man said. "I'll fill the tub. It'll be ready in about ten minutes."

Foxx wasted no time when he got into the bare but reasonably clean room. After lighting the lamp on the battered bureau, he shed his coat and hung it on one of the wall hooks beside the bed. His vest was next. He hung it on the back of the room's single chair after moving the chair to within easy reach of the bed. Unbuckling his gunbelt, he placed it on the seat of the chair with the holster of the Smith & Wesson where his hand would grasp it without groping.

Sitting on the side of the bed, Foxx pulled off his boots and socks. He stood up and was unbuttoning his shirt before he remembered that he and Pepper had left their saddlebags and rifles in the care of the liveryman. For a moment he weighed the comfort of having fresh underwear and a clean shirt to put on in the morning against the inconvenience of dressing again and walking all the way to the end of the settlement to get his gear, and in the end he decided the effort was not worth the reward.

Lighting a stogie, Foxx sat down on the side of the bed until he heard the night clerk's footsteps plodding back from the bathroom, then walked quickly down the hall in his underwear and had his bath. The cool water in the tub did not encourage dawdling. He soaped and rinsed quickly, felt the stubble on his jaws and resolved to find a barbershop right after breakfast, and went back to his room.

Looking at the bed, Foxx suddenly realized that he was very sleepy. He stepped out of his loose-fitting linen undersuit, turned back the bedclothes, blew out the lamp, and slipped between the threadbare sheets. The mattress had a few lumps in it, but Foxx had slept on lumpy mattresses before, and after a night on the hard ground and two long days in the saddle, the mattress felt as soft as a featherbed.

For a short time sleep evaded him, while his tired muscles adjusted to the uneven mattress and his ears to the raucous voices of drunken construction-camp workers going past the hotel after an evening spent amid the dubious pleasures of Hell on Wheels. Nothing could keep him awake very long. He slid into the stage between sleep and waking as the noises from outside diminished, then he quickly dropped off to sleep.

Although exhausted, he was awake instantly when the first faint sound came from the door. He did not identify the source of the noise until the doorknob rattled again. The noise was faint, but in the silence it sounded loud.

Foxx sat up, the S&W already in his hand by the time his head left the pillow. The room was dark, but the tattered window shade let a few bits of stray light from the outside trickle into the room. He waited, testing the silence of the sleeping hotel, thinking that perhaps some hotel guest seeking the bathroom had rattled his doorknob by mistake. The knob rattled again, this time a bit more insistently.

Foxx threw back the covers and padded noiselessly on his bare feet to the door. "Pepper?" he asked, his voice a half-whisper. "That you?"

There was no reply, and the doorknob remained quiet, but a soft grating noise followed his question as someone in the hallway scratched at the door panels.

"Pepper?" Foxx repeated.

A whisper reached Foxx's ears in response to his question, but the whisperer's voice was so low as to be unidentifiable, the words indistinguishable.

Foxx unlocked the door, the rasp of the key grating loudly in the stillness. He cracked the door open and peered through the slit. The hallway was unlighted, but a faint gleam crept down it from the lamp on the desk in the entry.

Foxx saw a silhouetted form, swathed in a dark garment, a coat or cloak, that made the dim figure unidentifiable. The thought struck him that his midnight caller might be someone seeking a former occupant of the room.

"Who in hell are you and who're you looking for?" he asked, holding the S&W poised in his hand.

A chuckle came from the shrouded figure, then a woman's voice replied, "I looked for a less suspicious welcome, Foxx."

Foxx recognized the voice at once, but his question was automatic. "Lita?"

"Of course. Were you expecting someone else?"

"I wasn't expecting nobody."

"If that is the case, then, why don't you open your door and invite me to come in?" she asked.

CHAPTER 8

"One reason is that I ain't got a stitch of clothes on," Foxx replied.

"I do not have eyes like a cat, Foxx," Lita replied, her voice carefully casual. "But if you want me to go—"

"No," Foxx answered quickly. "I don't guess you'd come looking for me at this time of night unless you had a pretty good reason. Now, if you don't mind standing in the dark a minute, I'll light the lamp soon as I pull on my britches."

He opened the door, standing behind it, while Lita came into the room. She stood aside to let Foxx close the door, and said nothing when she heard the grating of the lock as he turned the key. Foxx groped for his trousers on the wall hook beside the bed and stepped into them quickly. Matches were lying on the seat of the chair that held his gunbelt and stogies. Foxx laid the S&W on the seat, but did not return the gun to its holster. He found a match and struck it.

Lita had not moved. She stood against the wall at one side of the door, and by the wavering light of the match Foxx saw that she was wrapped in a dark high-collared cloak with a hood that came up over her head. An enigmatic smile flickered across her face as she saw him looking at her.

"Is it necessary that we have light?" she asked. "There are times when there is more truth to be found in the darkness."

"Whatever you say," Foxx replied, but before blowing out the match he picked up a stogie and lighted it.

Foxx was momentarily light-blinded when the match flame died, but the glow of the cigar enabled him to see dimly while his eyes adjusted. He could make out Lita's form as she moved to sit on the edge of the bed, at the foot. She let the cape slide off her shoulders and patted the bed beside her.

"Come and sit down, Foxx. But before you do, you might pour me a drink. I've had to swallow so much lukewarm tea tonight that I need something to kill its taste."

"I'd sure like to oblige you, Lita, but I'm fresh out of liquor. I got a bottle in my saddlebags, but they're down at the livery stable."

Lita said calmly, "I thought you might not be prepared to offer a visitor a drink, so I brought my own." She fumbled in the folds of the cloak, brought out a bottle, and handed it to Foxx. "The barkeeper told me this is the kind of whiskey you ordered at the saloon."

"Cyrus Noble?" Foxx asked, taking the bottle. His eyes had adjusted to the darkness now, but he could not make out the label. He felt around the cork, and his fingertips told him that the paper strip of the revenue stamp had not been tampered with. He tore off the stamp and jarred the cork loose with a quick thump on the bottom of the bottle, then worked the cork out with his fingers. He said, "I didn't look to see if there's a glass in this room."

"It doesn't matter, Foxx. A women can drink from a bottle as easily as a man."

Foxx handed Lita the bottle, and she tilted it to her lips. She drank and returned the bottle to Foxx. Now that she had taken the first swallow, Foxx did not hesitate but downed a healthy slug of the smooth bourbon. He was sure that Lita would have left him to drink alone if the liquor had been dosed with chloral hydrate.

She asked in a half-whisper, "Have you been wondering why I came to visit you tonight?"

"Two or three reasons come to mind right off," Foxx replied quickly. "Now, I don't aim to make you mad at me, or hurt your feelings, Lita, but maybe I better tell you right now how I feel about women. I like ladies just the same as I do good whiskey. I don't mind buying the whiskey, but I balk at buying a woman."

"I am not for sale," Lita replied. Her voice was level and showed neither anger not injured pride. "No man has enough money to buy me, Foxx. I am not a whore."

"Then I better apologize for what I said."

"No. You do not need to. I can understand why

you might have thought so, because of the work I do in the saloon. But my job there is dealing cards, nothing else."

"And you're real good at it, too."

"Not good enough to deceive you, though. You have quick eyes, Foxx."

"If we're going to tell each other the truth, Lita, I didn't see you switch that jack of diamonds. I've seen monte dealers pull that trick before, and I just lucked out when I picked the jack after you'd fixed the corner."

"There are times when luck is better than skill," she said.

For a moment they sat in silence, each of them waiting for the other to speak. Foxx puffed his cigar, and the brightened glow of its tip outlined Lita's features clearly, now that his eyes had grown accustomed to the darkness.

Her face was turned toward him, but he could not tell if her expression was amusement or anticipation. Lita's eyes were glowing like black coals below her thick, glossy brows, and her full, moist lips were parted in a half-smile. The low neck of the china poblana blouse had slipped down on one shoulder, and the deep cleft between her breasts showed as a dark shadow against the creamy whiteness of her skin.

When Foxx said nothing, Lita broke the silence before it became uncomfortable.

"I think I would like another sip of the whiskey." Foxx passed her the bottle, and after she'd swallowed and placed the bottle on the floor beside the bed, she went on, "You have not asked me why I came here. Do you know, or aren't you curious?"

"Oh, I'm curious as the next man." Foxx paused long enough to drop the butt of his stogie in the spittoon beside the bed. "You said you didn't come to sell me anything, and I sure ain't got nothing to sell you. That just leaves one reason, the way I see it." Foxx stopped short.

"And the reason?" Lita's voice challenged him.

"When a pretty young lady calls on a man in his room in the middle of the night, it ain't likely she's there to ask him to help her say her prayers."

Lita's laugh tinkled through the darkened room. Then, the challenge in her voice even more explicit, she asked, "And so?"

"And so we might as well start not praying," Foxx replied, bending to kiss her.

Lita responded with a questing tongue that thrust between Foxx's lips and twined itself around his. Foxx's hand caressed her warm, bare shoulder, and she shrugged to free her other shoulder from the loose blouse, which slipped down to her waist.

Foxx cupped one of the freed breasts in his hand and felt its tip budding to firmness as he stroked the warm globe. Their breath exhausted by the prolonged kiss, their lips drew apart, and Foxx bent his head to run the tip of his tongue around Lita's outthrust nipples.

He was already beginning to grow hard when Lita slid a soft hand into the unbuttoned fly of his trousers. She grasped him and began gently squeezing him, her hand warm as she caressed him. The pulsing of her squeezes speeded up as Foxx's tongue traced a moist path over her breasts, and his erection swelled quickly to full hardness. He stopped now and then to take the tips of her budded rosettes between his teeth and nip them gently. Lita began to squirm, moving her torso from side to side, arching her back to tighten the skin of her heaving breasts.

She was now encircling Foxx firmly with one hand while with the other she fumbled at the single button that he'd fastened at the waistband of his trousers. She worked at the buttonhole until the button yielded, and pulled his fly open to free his erection. Without interrupting the attention she was giving to the firm, upthrust cylinder she'd liberated, Lita raised her free hand to rub it across Foxx's bare chest and then to stroke the softer skin of his shoulders and back.

Foxx's head was still bent forward as his mouth moved over her heaving breasts. Lita shifted her position until her cheek was on Foxx's shoulder, and ran her warm, wet lips along it until they reached the soft arch at the base of his neck, and Foxx felt the tip of her tongue begin to explore the pulsing hollow. She continued the caress while he moved his lips across her breasts, stopping at their firm, hard tips to draw them into his mouth, where his tongue could move across the tips and the budded rosettes surrounding them.

By now both Foxx and Lita were gasping for breath, and when Lita lifted her head and fell back on the mattress, Foxx released her and stood up beside the bed. He let his trousers fall and stepped out of them. Lita raised her hips and pushed her blouse and her billowing, full skirt and petticoats down to her thighs. With a kick and a wriggle of her broad hips, she freed her legs of the garments and kicked them to the floor.

She wore nothing under the skirts, and the black triangle of her pubic brush made a wide vee below the tautness of her stomach as she parted her thighs and gasped, "Don't make me wait any longer, Foxx! Give me what I came looking for!"

Foxx moved between the invitingly spread thighs, and Lita wrapped her legs around him. She pulled him down and guided him into her. Foxx felt the hot wetness of Lita's second lips spread to welcome him as he thrust down hard and swiftly, until his groin was pressed against her smooth, yielding belly and he was buried fully inside her with no more left to give.

Lita's hips were writhing against him, and Foxx held himself motionless while she squirmed and panted for a few moments; then he began stroking with long, steady penetrations. Lita's body tensed and her back arched. Each time Foxx lunged into her, she closed her thighs around his hips and clung to him for a moment, trying to pull him deeper. Foxx's eyes could penetrate the darkness now. He watched Lita's face under his, her lips working and her eyes squeezed shut, her head pressed back on the bed to bring her neck up in an arch while she strained against him.

Then, before Foxx could slow the tempo of his stroking, Lita suddenly began shaking furiously. Her mouth opened to release a stream of moaning sighs which trailed away into silence as her passion faded from convulsive upheavals to a ripple of relaxation. She sighed and lay quietly beneath him. Foxx stopped thrusting when he felt Lita's spasm ending. He pressed firmly into her while the small shudders were fading, then relaxed and lay as motionless as she was.

Lita opened her eyes and looked up at him. "I'm sorry I had to let go too soon, Foxx. I wanted to wait for you, but I just couldn't hold back."

"Don't let that bother you. I got enough steam left to last us awhile yet."

"I hope you have." Lita worked her hips from side to side in slow tentative motions, pushing up against him as she moved. "Yes. I can tell you do, from the way you feel inside of me, just as big and hard as when we started."

"And ready to go whenever you are," Foxx assured her. "But I can wait till you're ready to start again."

"I don't want to wait," she told him and proved it by lifting her hips to press against him.

Foxx responded immediately. He started stroking again, long, slow lunges that brought soft, ecstatic gasps from Lita, who began to meet his thrusts with a gentle rocking of her hips. Foxx paced himself as her fervor increased. He waited until her gentle rocking became violent upheavals and then allowed himself to build, lunging deeper and faster to meet Lita's growing frenzy. The soft moans which had started her first climax began streaming from her throat.

Then he drove even harder, speeding up as his own orgasm began. When he felt Lita begin to tremble, out of control, he let his body take over from his mind and joined her in a final quaking spasm that peaked with a burst of frantic thrusting and heaving, and then their peaks passed and they lay quietly.

After a while Lita said softly, "I knew from the

minute I saw you tonight that you'd be a good lover, Foxx."

"You know a lot of moves yourself, Lita. Things you didn't find out just by dealing three-card monte."

"Things I enjoy sharing with the right man," she said. "I don't pay a visit to every man I see across a monte layout."

"Well, I'm glad you picked me out."

Foxx groped on the chair until he'd found a stogie and match, and lighted the short, twisted cigar. He picked up the bottle of Cyrus Noble from the floor, where Lita had placed it, and offered it to her.

She shook her head. "No more for me. I'll have to go soon, as much as I'd like to stay longer."

Foxx drank and put the bottle down. "I got to get a few winks of sleep, too. There's a lot of work waiting for me."

"From what Pepper said, I know you both work for the C&K, and I got the idea you're in charge of some kind of special job."

"It ain't all that special, Lita. I just go where they tell me to."

"Doing what?"

"I guess you'd call me a kind of troubleshooter."

"What kind of trouble?"

"Oh, there's lots of different kinds of trouble that need to be straightened out when you work for a railroad."

Lita's brows drew together. "I know there's been trouble here and at La Paz with men attacking the work crews."

"There's been some raids, sure. Everybody knows that."

"But nobody seems to know who's been doing the raiding. And I don't suppose you've been here long enough to've learned much about them, have you?"

"We didn't get here until an hour or so before Pepper walked into that saloon you work at."

"But that is the trouble you were sent to straighten out, isn't it, Foxx?"

Again Foxx avoided a direct answer. He said casually, "Well, trouble's trouble, Lita. I take on all kinds of odd jobs."

"You are going to be here awhile, though?" she asked. "At least long enough for us to be together again?"

"That's hard to say right now. It depends on how long it takes me to finish the job I got to do."

"Will I see you tomorrow night?" she asked eagerly. "Or, I guess I ought to say tonight, it's so late."

"I ain't sure. I move around a lot, so I never know much ahead of time where I'm likely to be. If I'm here tomorrow night, I'll show up at the saloon and see how you feel about me by then."

"You know how I feel about you now. Don't expect me to change between tonight and tomorrow." Lita bent to kiss Foxx, a long good-bye kiss that only his determination kept from turning into something even more prolonged. She got out of bed and bent to gather up her clothing. Dressing was a simple matter of pulling the china poblana blouse over her head and stepping into her skirt. "I'll look for you at the saloon, then," she told Foxx, brushing his lips with hers.

"If I'm back in time," he said. "But if I don't make it tonight, or even tomorrow, I'll be in soon as I can."

Already at the door, Lita said over her shoulder, "Sooner, Foxx. I'll be waiting for you."

After the small thuds of Lita's light footsteps going down the hall had faded into silence, Foxx got up and locked the door. He stretched out on the bed, but he couldn't fall asleep. Lighting a fresh stogie, he reached for the bottle of Cyrus Noble, smoked until gray dawn light showed around the edges of the tattered shade at the room's single window. Even when he finally fell asleep, he had not evolved a plan that satisfied him completely.

"Damn it, Foxx, I thought you said we was going to take it sorta easy today," Pepper said. "Now you got some wild hair up your ass, and here we are getting ready to ride off to God knows where, looking for who knows what!"

Since breakfast, which they'd eaten late in the morning, when he'd told Pepper they were changing plans and riding out, Pepper had been trying to find out what had caused Foxx to change his mind and where they were going. Foxx had remained silent, and Pepper had been chaffering about being kept in the dark.

"We know what we're looking for," Foxx replied. "And we got a pretty good idea where to look, or will have when we pick up that trail we quit on yesterday."

While he talked, Foxx kept his eyes on the liveryman, who had finished saddling one of the horses Foxx had rented, and was tightening the cinch on the second. He fumbled in his coat pocket for a cigar before remembering that he'd left his coat hanging in his hotel room. That had meant leaving his Pailliard repeater watch behind, too, since he needed his vest pockets for the items usually distributed between coat and vest. He had not left his Colt Cloverleaf in the room but had stuffed it into his boot top, where it made an almost invisible bulge with its cylinder set in its flat configuration.

"You told me you wanted to stay here today and talk to Pat Riley." Pepper frowned. "Why'd you change your mind?"

"Because I had plenty of reason to," Foxx replied curtly. "I decided I'd talked to Pat enough last night to do me for a space. Now, don't get riled up, Pepper. I'll tell you all the whys and wherefores soon enough."

"Well, you're the boss." Pepper sighed. "If you say frog, I guess it's my place to hop."

"I ain't trying to be a tough boss," Foxx told the unhappy Pepper. "You oughta know that by now." The liveryman gave the cinch a final tug and handed the reins to Foxx, who went on, "Just straddle your nag, now, and let's get moving."

As they left Hell on Wheels behind and turned their horses to follow the perimeter of the construction camp, Pepper voiced one last complaint. "I sure as hell hope you got enough grub to see us through whatever kind of wild-goose chase we're going on."

"I got enough to last us four days. Which is more'n we're likely to need. I figure this ain't going to be more'n a two-day trip, three at the outside."

Pepper subsided then. He said nothing but showed that his feelings had been hurt by Foxx's refusal to explain all the aspects of their mission by holding his horse in, so that instead of riding abreast as he had always done on their earlier trip, he was always a few yards in the rear. Foxx matched his reluctant companion's stubborn silence until they were well away from the construction camp; then he turned and motioned to Pepper to ride up abreast.

"I don't blame you for getting riled," he told the feisty little man. "But I had to keep my mouth shut until we got outa Hell on Wheels because in a place like that a man never can be sure who's listening to what he says, or who they'll repeat it to."

"You saying I been talking too much?" Pepper demanded.

"Damn it, Pepper, cool off!" Foxx snapped. "It ain't you I'm talking about. I'm trying to tell you where we're heading and what we're aiming to do, if you'll just let me get on with it!"

"You mean you've found out there's somebody in Hell on Wheels that's been talking around about us?"

"Not exactly talking. More like asking questions."

"Well, why didn't we just go after the son of a bitch and shut him up?"

"It ain't all that easy," Foxx replied.

In as few words as possible, and omitting as much personal details as he could, Foxx gave Pepper a greatly censored version of Lita's visit. He wasn't yet sure that the suspicions created in his mind by her questions the night before were justified, and he wanted to avoid giving Pepper the impression that he was being blamed for having been the unwitting link between the girl and their job.

"So I guess you see now why I didn't want to say anything about where we might be going or how long we'd be gone. If that Lita was trying to find out to tip off them night riders, there's likely to be others in Hell on Wheels, or even in Pat Riley's work crews, that'd do the same thing."

"Spies, you mean?" Pepper asked. "By God, Foxx, that sounds just like there was a war going on, instead of a gang of robbers riding in to shoot up a construction camp!"

"Maybe them night riders take it to be a war," Foxx replied soberly. He shook his head and added, "You called them men robbers, Pepper. You ever hear of anything they stole?"

Pepper's face drew into a thoughtful scowl. "Now, when you come right up to taw, I never did."

"I never did, either. That fellow the other night kept harping on the Santa Maria River bridge, so it seems to me like that's got more to do with them raids than just plain robbing. And none of the reports Frank Sanders sent to the main office ever said a word about any of them raiders doing any looting."

"You make it sound like there's more'n one gang," Pepper said, his voice puzzled.

"For all we know now, there might be. That's one of the things we're going to try to find out."

"Well, I can see now why you was so hush-mouthed about us riding out today," Pepper told Foxx.

Foxx realized that was as close as his helper could come to apologizing, and nodded in acknowledgment. "Let's don't worry about what's over with, Pepper. We'll just go ahead and do our jobs, like we're supposed to."

They rode on through the bright midday sunshine, Pepper moving up now to ride abreast of

Foxx. In midafternoon they reached the river. Foxx examined the hoofprints their horses had made when they rode north; the prints were undisturbed, as clear as if they'd been made minutes earlier. He nodded with satisfaction, thinking that the trail they were going to be following should be equally clear.

After they'd crossed the Bill Williams River, Foxx reined in beside the manure pile that had been his first clue to the night riders' ruse in continuing so far upriver. Unlike the hoofprints, the horse droppings had changed in the hot sun. They were no longer a fresh dark brown but had faded to a bleached tan. They already looked dry, and in another day, Foxx knew they would be faded to almost the same hue as that of the gravel bed on which they lay.

"We'll circle the gravel," he told Pepper. "There's got to be tracks left in the soft dirt where it gives out."

Very little time was required for them to find the trail they were seeking. Pepper spotted the hoofprints on their first circuit of the gravel bed.

"That looks like the ones we're after," he said, excitement stirring in his voice as he pointed to the deep crescents a few dozen yards from the point where the hard gravel which began at the river started to become a mixture of rocks and soil and then gave way completely to soft dirt. "What d'you think, Foxx?"

Foxx glanced at the prints briefly and nodded. "It's them, all right.

"How in hell can you tell that?" Pepper asked. "You didn't look at them hoofprints for more'n half a second."

"I told you, I learned a little bit of tracking when I was a young un," Foxx replied. "I'll tell you something else, Pepper. Wherever their hideout is, it ain't real far away from here."

"What makes you so damn sure?" Pepper challenged.

"Stands to reason. There ain't no kind of marked path or road of any kind, but they cut straight as a string to wherever it is they hole up. All five of 'em left us at the same time, and they didn't have no way of knowing whether we'd try to take after 'em, so they must've knowed they could get to where they'd be safe by the time we picked up their trail. I'll bet we'll find their hideout less than ten miles from here."

"Now, just how much of a bet you want to make on that?"

"Tell you what, Pepper. I'll bet you a bottle of Noble I'm right all down the line," Foxx replied. "Now let's quit jawing and start moving! I want to see that hideout before dark!"

CHAPTER 9

As they followed the trail of the group that had intruded on their camp, Foxx was grateful—and not for the first time—to the merciless Comanche teachers who'd demanded perfection in tracking from their youthful pupils. By the time he and Pepper had been riding for an hour, he had a clear picture in his mind of the party they were tracking.

Not only could Foxx recognize the individual hoofprints of each of the five horses, but he was confident that if he was given a bit more time to study them he could estimate to within a few pounds the weight of the animals that made the tracks, which would give him an indication of their size. He was sure, too, that he would also be able to identify the riders on each horse if he saw them in the saddle, even if they'd changed mounts.

Patterns made by the hoofprints told Foxx that one of the men they were trailing might handle the reins with a hard hand on the near side, which meant that the man might be left-handed or inclined to favor that hand or arm. Another of the riders let his reins go slack, or did not use them as often as needed; his mount did not move in a straight path but veered from one side to the other. Almost imperceptible differences in the depth of the prints left by a third horse revealed that the man riding it put most of his weight on one side of the saddle, or rode with badly adjusted stirrups, for the prints showed that the horse consistently wandered to the left side of the trail. He noticed no peculiarities about the remaining two riders but was sure that, given time, he could find a pattern to the prints that would allow him to recognize their riders as well.

Foxx did not tell Pepper of the conclusions he'd reached about their quarry; he did not want his concentration on the tracks interrupted by having to explain his deductions. So they wasted no time in talk but forged ahead steadily, making their way from the relatively verdant area bordering the Bill Williams River into country that grew progressively drier, more rugged, and more broken.

They were in the hundred-mile-wide transition zone in which Arizona Territory's landscape changed from grassy foothills and mountains to the barren desert that covered the land down to the Mexican border. Little of it had been explored by men who had left records of the geographical features they'd encountered. To newcomers like Foxx and Pepper, the area was as new as the face of the moon.

Soon the narrow alluvial strip gave way to a series of slitlike canyons. The tracks they were following, which had veered only a little from the string-straight line in which they'd led from the river, now began to zigzag between these oversized gullies. A few of them were narrow enough for the horses to jump, but more often a detour had to be made around the mouth of one of the gulches, or else they had to ride along the canyon's rim until they reached a point where it was narrow enough for the horses to leap across.

All the zigzagging they'd been forced to do had eaten up time. Neither Foxx or Pepper had been hungry at noon because of their late breakfast, and because of Foxx's certainty that the gang's hideout was close by they'd delayed stopping to eat until the afternoon was well along. Measured in a straight line, the distance they'd covered from the spot where they'd picked up the trail was very short. When Foxx suddenly reined in, the sun was well down in the sky, and they were crossing a long, level mesa.

"We better begin looking around a lot more and be real sure of what's ahead of us," he told Pepper. "We're getting close to the hideout now."

"How in hell do you figure that?"

Foxx pointed to the tracks. "The bunch we're after begun to slow down as soon as they got to the top of this mesa. Right along here they slowed up a lot more."

"You're reading that in them hoofprints we been following?" Pepper asked, staring at the tracks, trying to interpret them for himself.

"If you know what to look for, you can tell a lot more than the direction somebody taken by the tracks they left. Now, back there a ways you could see the prints wasn't as deep and they wasn't spaced so far apart. They'd stopped pushing the horses—not that they ever did try to make real good time."

"Well, we ain't been in much of a hurry ourselves," Pepper pointed out.

"I'll grant you that. You never can move quite as fast as the ones you're tracking, Pepper," Foxx explained. "It's taken us maybe an hour longer to cover this much territory than it did the bunch we're trailing. That's because they knew right where they were headed, and we've had to go slower because we haven't ever been sure whether the trail was going to zig or zag."

"You figure we're getting close to their hidey-hole now, though?"

"Pretty close, I'd say. We might be as much as two or three miles away from it, but I'll lay you odds we ain't much further."

"Not me, you won't!" Pepper grinned. "Looks like I already stand to lose that bet we made back where we started off. You won't catch me making no more bets with a man that's got eyes sharp as yours is."

Even with the advantage that being mounted gave them in surveying the terrain ahead, and in spite of Foxx's careful tracking, the wide canyon that split the mesa took them by surprise. They rode up a hump, and suddenly the canyon yawned in front of them, a gap that was a mile or more across. The hump had concealed it from them; until they'd reached its top, the land beyond looked as though the mesa's surface continued uninterrupted. They had reined in by instinct when they saw the gap so close ahead. Now they toed their horses forward at a walk until they reached the canyon's rim and could look into its depths.

What they looked down upon was worthy of comparison with the European castles of centuries long past. There was no apparent sign of life in or around the huge structure, although it showed no obvious signs of decay either. The building looked enormous from the height where Foxx and Pepper were. Its walls were smoothly plastered, adobe-brown, and tall, square turrets at each corner rose above its central section. The turrets were massive structures themselves, with walls that sloped upward from the ground at an angle too steep to be scaled, without a handhold or foothold for the first thirty or forty feet of their height, after which tall window slits broke their smoothness.

The central structure sprawled like an enormous rectangular box. Its walls sloped upward, too, and the first windows that pierced them were also narrow slits. Much higher above ground, at the level of a second or even a third story, there were wider windows. All the windows were embrasured; the wooden shutters that covered them were set deeply into walls that Foxx judged were at least four to five feet thick even at their tops.

"Well, I'll be damned!" Foxx said as they looked down at the canyon's floor. "Who'd ever expect to see something like that in a place like this!"

"I sure as hell wouldn't," Pepper agreed. "Why, that looks like some pictures I seen in a book one time. They showed a lot of old-time castles from over across the ocean in Europe. You know, the kind of castles that kings and dukes and all them fancy folks lived in away back when."

"It does, at that." Foxx nodded. "And for all we know, it might've been built a hundred years or more ago by some of them settlers that begun coming up here when Mexico still belonged to Spain. I forget how long ago they started settling north of the Rio Grande, but it was two or three hundred years back."

"All I can say is, it looks to me like a mighty spooky place," Pepper commented as Foxx instinctively leaned forward, trying to see as much as he could.

In the two walls of the building that were visible Foxx saw no doors. The roofs of both the main part of the vast building and the turrets were made of dull-red semicylindrical tiles that glowed with the patina of the years.

Foxx turned his attention from the building to the canyon in which it stood. The canyon's sheer walls dropped a hundred yards to its floor, and at the widest part, where the building stood, a quarter of a mile lay between it and the canyon walls. The canyon was shaped like an egg, with one end more sharply tapering than the other. The building was not in the center of the canyon but closer to the narrow end. From where Foxx and Pepper had stopped, there was no visible sign of a passage into the canyon at either end.

"It sure must've taken a lot of men a lot of time to put up a building like that," Pepper said, shaking his head.

"I'd say a lot of people lived around it awhile

back," Foxx told him. "Servants and the like, I imagine."

He pointed to the crumbling remains of small houses, little more than huts, which stood in a semicircle behind the huge edifice. A ditch which must once have carried water divided the area where the small houses had stood into two quadrants; the ancient acequia was totally dry, though.

"You reckon that big palace is where them night riders holes up?" Pepper asked.

"More likely than not," Foxx replied. "The trail we been following is bound to lead down to the floor. And if you look close, you'll see what's left of an old wagon road that runs south, toward the narrow part. That'd give 'em a way in and out at both ends of the canyon."

Pepper looked where Foxx pointed and said, "Old wagon roads don't mean much in Arizona Territory. Most of 'em don't go anywhere no more. Hell, there wasn't a railroad west of the Mississippi when the Mexicans settled here, and they owned this part of the country a long time before we taken it in '46."

"As close as I can tell, that road down there ain't had a wagon on it for a long time. All the ruts is just about blown smooth," Foxx said. "Far as I can see, it's the only road leading out of the canyon, but we'll know more about that after we go down and look at it."

"We're going to go down there?"

"That's what we come for, ain't it? To find the place where them night riders hole up?"

"Well, sure," Pepper admitted. "But you can tell that it sure ain't a big place like that one down there.

Anyhow, I don't see no smoke coming up from anywheres, which there'd be if anybody was using it or living there."

"We've got to look, just the same, smoke or no smoke," Foxx said. "It could be the place we're looking for, and the gang might be away, pulling another one of their raids."

"If we're going down there, we better get cracking, then," Pepper said. "Damn it, I feel bare-ass naked sitting here, Foxx. If there's anybody inside of that place, all they got to do is look outa one of them windows, and here we are. Hadn't we oughta be scouting around to find that trail you said has to go down into that canyon?"

"I don't imagine it'll take much scouting," Foxx replied. "All we got to do is keep following these hoofprints. We'll see real fast that they'll lead us down to the bottom."

His prediction was correct. They followed the hoofprints on to the rim, and there they saw a shelved path that led to the canyon floor. With Foxx leading the way, they started down. The trail bore the hoofprints of many horses, showing it was in regular use. It was surprisingly easy despite its continuous downward slant, and even the corners where the path cut back on itself did not slow their progress appreciably.

As they rode down the shelved path, Foxx soon understood why their descent was so easy. At the corner of one of the first cutbacks he saw the marks of picks and mattocks on the canyon wall, where men had widened and leveled the path. The walls beside the trail also showed signs of incised grooves left by the earth-working tools where the naturally narrow spots had been widened and the grades made easier. Though he looked at the tool marks closely, he was unable to judge whether they were old or recent. In that land of small and infrequent rains the marks would have remained clear and sharp-edged for many years.

Within little more than a quarter of an hour after they'd started down, they rode onto the floor of the canyon. The tracks they were following were clear-cut in the softer earth of the canyon floor. They led along the western wall of the canyon, and Foxx could see that the men they'd been trailing had ridden between the wall of the canyon and the castle.

Seen from the ground near its base, the huge building looked even more impressively massive than it had from above. It dominated the level canyon floor, and whether they were looking at it or away from it, Foxx and Pepper were always conscious of the high walls and even higher turrets looming above them. They reined in a hundred yards away from the building and sat looking up at it.

"Damn! It's bigger'n it looks from up above!" Pepper said.

"It's that, all right," Foxx agreed. "It'll take awhile just to ride around it, let alone look inside."

"Maybe we better split up to save time," Pepper suggested. "You go around it one way, I'll go the other, and we'll meet in front of it."

Foxx shook his head. "No. We'll split up to be safe, but both of us ain't going close to that place at the same time. You stay here, Pepper, and sorta act a sentry. I'll ride around it and see what I can find out."

Sliding his Winchester out of its scabbard, Foxx

levered a fresh shell into the chamber. He caught the cartridge that was ejected, looked at its base for signs of oil, found none, and slid the shell into the magazine. Laying the rifle across the pommel of his saddle, he nudged his horse with a foot, and the animal started toward the castle at a slow walk.

As Foxx rounded a corner of the towering edifice, he got his first look at its eastern side. There, cut into the center of the wall, was the first and only door he'd seen in the building.

It was a massive portal, with double doors tall enough for a man on horseback to pass under them and wide enough for two riders to go through them side by side. The well-weathered surface of the twin doors bore many scars. They looked as if they had withstood the hacking of axes more than once but showed no signs they had ever been breached. Foxx could see no tracks leading to or from the doorway, so he did not stop to inspect it at close range but rode on toward the end of the building.

He swung out to go around the base of the corner turret, and as he rounded the outthrust buttress that extended from the castle's main wall, he heard a strange wailing behind him, as though some wild animal was crying harshly. Almost as soon as the wailing noise sounded, Foxx realized it was the rasping of the hinges on the door he'd just passed.

He turned in his saddle to look behind him, got a glimpse of movement out of the corner of his eye as he did so, and tried to reverse to see what had caught his attention. His move was a fraction of a second too late. A man holding a rifle now stood at the turret's sloping base. The gun was leveled at Foxx.

"Estay steel!" the man commanded harshly. He raised the rifle's muzzle until Foxx was looking down the black bore of the gun and said, "Let eet fall, *el fusil, inmediatamente!*"

Foxx stared blankly at the man, giving no indication that he had understood the order. He knew that to try to bring his own rifle around would be to write his death sentence. He heard hoofbeats coming up from behind him but did not risk turning to look.

"Talk English," he began. "I don't—"

"*¡Cállate!*" the man interrupted. "*¡Deja el fusil, o tiro!*"

To underline his commands to Foxx to keep silent and drop his gun, the man with the rifle let off a shot. Foxx winced as the slug whistled uncomfortably close to his head. He knew from the increasing loudness of the hoofbeats behind him that his time for action was ticking away fast, but he could not risk moving. He kept his eyes fixed on the threatening rifleman.

Time ran out. A horse's head brushed past Foxx's leg, then the body of the horse scraped against him, twisting his leg and pushing his foot out of the stirrup. Rough hands grabbed him and pulled the rifle from his grasp. Foxx turned to look at the rider. He did not recognize the man's wide, flat face, brown with slitted obsidian eyes set in an almost Mongolian slant.

Tossing Foxx's Winchester to the ground, the rider leaned across Foxx's chest to pull the Smith & Wesson out of its cross-draw holder. Foxx grasped the man's extended arm and tried to pull him off his horse, but he was already badly off-balance himself from the weight of the other's body pushing him backward and sidewise.

Foxx began to slide out of the saddle, pulling his assailant with him, but the livery horse began bucking. He felt his grip slipping. The attacker got the butt of the S&W in his hand, drew it, and clubbed Foxx. Half-stunned, Foxx relaxed his hold. He toppled to the ground. The last thing he was aware of was a scattering of distant shots from behind the castle.

Consciousness returned to Foxx slowly. For the first few seconds of returning awareness he did not recall everything that had happened. But a warning signal flashed in his mind, telling him to be careful of what he did. Foxx waited, trying to regain control of himself. He kept his eyes closed, absorbing his sensations and fixing his position. He felt the rough pebble-strewn earth on his back and under his outstretched hands and realized that he was lying on the ground. His head was pulsing but did not hurt him too badly. The brim of his hat had broken the impact of the blow he'd taken. He remembered that he had heard shooting behind the castle just before blacking out and recalled vaguely wondering what had happened to Pepper.

With that memory the reality of his situation flooded back fully into Foxx's mind. He opened his eyes and saw two sets of horse's legs and two of human legs standing beside him. He moved his gaze upward and saw the rifleman who'd first stopped him, then, with a burst of surprise that he managed to conceal, recognized the second man. He was the poker player whom Foxx had first encountered in the

La Paz saloon where the affray with the Mexican had taken place.

"*No está dañado, Alvarez,*" the rifleman said when he saw Foxx's eyes opened. "*Puede andar en la hacienda.*"

"*Creo que sí,*" the other answered. He poked his toe into Foxx's ribs. "To the feet, now, Foxx! We are to go eenside."

Foxx could not hide the surprise that showed on his face when Alvarez called him by name; then he remembered that the man had heard him identify himself to the barkeep in La Paz. He took his time getting to his feet, moving with exaggerated unsteadiness, and made no protest when the man with the rifle prodded him around to face Alvarez.

"*Bueno,*" Alvarez said. "You weel follow now in back of me. Make no queek move, or Chato weel keel you!"

Realizing that arguing or resisting would be wasting time and effort at this point, Foxx obeyed. He was still wondering about Pepper's fate, but no more shots were being fired behind the castle, and he concluded that his helper was either dead or captured, though the fleeting thought that the feisty little man might have escaped flashed through his mind.

Foxx had decided instantly that his own problems had to be solved before he could give much thought to Pepper, and that he would probably get some answers inside the building. Moving as though he was still groggy, he shuffled forward. Chato moved with him, and Foxx felt the muzzle of the rifle pushed into the small of his back.

Leading the horses, Alvarez started around the base

of the corner turret. Prodded by Chato's rifle muzzle, Foxx followed. As they reached a point where he could see the north wall of the castle, a pair of oversized doors similar to those he'd passed on the building's side yawned open. Alvarez led the horses through the doors, and Foxx followed into the dim cavernous interior.

A lantern hanging on a wall bracket did little to dispel the semidarkness; the farthest reaches of the room were veiled in gloom. What little Foxx could see was clearly used as a stable. Stalls filled the center of the earthen floor, and still more lined the walls on both sides. There were horses in most of the stalls. A pump rose from the floor at one end of the center stalls, with a long watering trough below its spigot. Piles of loose hay stood just inside the open doors.

Alvarez guided the horses into empty stalls and returned to where Foxx and Chato stood. He had stuck Foxx's S&W into the waistband of his trousers. Now he took it out and said, *"Cierra las puertas, Chato, hasta que vuelvan Stenache y Eusebio con el otro Yanqui. Después llívalo en el piso de arriba. ¿Entiendes?"*

"Si, Alvarez. entiendo," Chato replied and started back toward the doorway.

Foxx understood enough of the instructions Alvarez had given to know that Pepper had not been captured yet, or if captured, had not been brought in. He kept his face impassive; one of the few cards he still held was his ability to understand much of what his captors said, and he intended to keep that card hidden.

Alvarez waited until Chato had started to close the doors, then returned his attention to Foxx. He said,

"Ees a stairs where estop the stalls. We are to go up eet. I owe you already the death for wheen you eshoot Raoul Morales. He was *buen compañero*. Eef you make try to escape, I am see you are to get queek bullet. You onderstan?"

"I understand, all right, Alvarez. And I ain't no more anxious to die than the next man. I won't try nothing."

"Oh, you weel estay alive." Alvarez chuckled. "So long as we find use of you. Then, wheen we are ready, *Yanqui*, you die!"

CHAPTER 10

Alvarez stood waiting for Foxx to reply to his threat, and when Foxx stayed silent, the night rider seemed disappointed. He said, "So. You esay nothing, no? When ees time come for you to die, I weel esee how brave you are." He motioned that Foxx was to move toward the center of the basementlike room. "*Ahora vamanos*. Are others waiting for you to talk."

Foxx started walking in the direction his captor had indicated. He did not have to look behind him to know the other man was following; Alvarez's footsteps whispered along in time with Foxx's on the packed earth. They had gone past the stalls and were near the end of the circle of light cast by the lantern before he saw the stairway, a straight flight of wooden steps.

Foxx started up the stairs, his ears tuned to Alvarez's position. The Indian had evidently anticipated Foxx's plan, or had been tricked before in a similar situation, for he kept so close behind that Foxx had no chance to lash back with a kick.

Foxx reached the top step. Alvarez pushed the muzzle of the S&W into his back and said, "Ees door. Open eet."

After a moment of fumbling, Foxx found the latch and pushed the door open. Coming from the dimness of the cellar, he was dazzled by the light in the long narrow room he entered. The window shutters, closed when he and Pepper first saw the castle, had been opened to the descending sun, which now hung just above the rim of the canyon and flooded the room with brilliance.

Foxx looked around. The room extended about a third of the length of the castle, as best as he could judge. Its walls were plastered in white, and red tiles covered the floor. In addition to the door through which Foxx and Alvarez entered, another door stood at the far end. The room was virtually bare of furniture; it contained only three sofas and a half-dozen chairs lined up along the inner wall.

Four men were sitting in the center of the chamber. They turned when the door opened, and one of them made a motion to rise, but the man next to him waved him back to his chair. They stared at Foxx with hard-set faces, and he could almost smell the hatred that seeped from their eyes and filled the narrow room.

Foxx was careful to let his own features show no expression at all as he looked from one to another of the quartet. All of them were dressed in much the same kind of clothing worn by Alvarez and Chato; brown duck jeans, loose denim jackets, and wide-brimmed hats. One of them wore a gunbelt with two holstered revolvers, the others carried only one pistol apiece. From what Foxx had observed since arriving in La Paz, the four men typified the racial mixture that he'd come to expect to see anywhere in Arizona Territory.

Only one of the men was Anglo-Saxon, though at first glance Foxx had taken him to be of Spanish or Mexican ancestry. His face and hands were tanned so deeply that his complexion was darker than that of two of his companions. A fringe of sandy hair and eyebrows bleached almost white by the sun were the only hints to his Anglo-Saxon origin.

A strong strain of pure Spanish blood showed in the features of the man sitting next to him. This one had a straight, high-bridged nose with flaring nostrils, thin lips and indrawn cheeks, and a long, slender jutting jaw. He was the slightest in build of the four, so thin that he seemed almost fragile.

Both the others had the wide faces, heavy jaws, and blunt features that marked them as Indians, and Foxx's mind went back for a flashing moment to his Comanche days. After Murate's band of Kotsotekas had killed his parents and forcibly adopted him, and Foxx had become a member of Ekhemurawa's family, he had gone several times with the tribe to the Valley of Tears. There had usually been Apaches visiting the Comanchero trading camps, and he needed only to look at the pair before him now to identify them as either half- or full-blood Apaches.

One of the Apaches was the first to speak. He asked Alvarez, "*¿Dónde está el otro?*"

"Eusebio y Stenache fueron por él, y ya no vuelven," Alvarez replied.

Reminded of Pepper by the question, Foxx remembered that the shooting he'd heard before being knocked out had been very brief and scattered. For a hopeful moment he thought that since the pair attacking him had not returned, Pepper might have escaped. Then, almost angry with himself for such wishful thinking, he told himself there was a greater probability that Pepper had been killed. The other Apache spoke and broke Foxx's train of thought.

"Será jubilosa, la francesa," he said to Alvarez. *"Ahorita tendrá uno nuevo a chingar, y a mi ver que éste tiene cojones como toro."*

Alvarez grunted. *"¡Maldita sea la francesa, Guevavi! Esto, ella se usa solamente poco tiempo, después toca a mí. Es el mismo quien mató a Morales a La Paz."*

Foxx held his face immobile, hiding his confusion over the meaning of this exchange. The reference to a Frenchwoman and the comparison of his sexual equipment to that of a bull made no sense to him. All that he'd understood clearly was Alvarez's remark about the killing in the La Paz saloon.

He was still trying to put the puzzle together when the stairway door opened and two men rushed in; Foxx concluded they were the pair who had been sent after Pepper. Everyone, Foxx included, turned to look at them. One of the newcomers was Apache, the other Foxx took to be an Apache-Spanish breed. He had little time to study them, for Alvarez spoke quickly.

"¿Qué le pasó al Yanqui?" Alvarez asked, visibly upset and worried.

"*Huyó*," the breed said, his voice just above a whisper.

"*¿Cómo es posible?*" Alvarez demanded. "*¡Dígame, Eusebio!*"

Before Eusebio could reply, the door at the far end of the room swung open, drawing all eyes in that direction. It was an oddly assorted pair who came hurrying in, despite a similarity in their clothing. The man in the lead was little larger than a teenaged youth, though as he came closer Foxx saw that he was in his middle twenties, at least. He had obsidian-black Apache eyes and full, thick Apache lips in a thin Spanish face. The man who followed him was big enough to be called a giant, and the contour of his face as well as his features marked him as pure Apache.

Both men had on charro suits—waist-length jackets and flared-cuff trousers. The jacket of the small man in the lead was so elaborately embroidered in gold that the tan fabric was almost completely hidden. Under the jacket he wore an ornate ruffled shirt. Foxx was surprised when he saw that although it was only late afternoon, and they were indoors, the small man was wearing fawn-colored gloves. The big man's outfit was without adornment of any kind, his trousers and jacket a somber shade of brown.

"Eusebio! Stenache!" the small man exclaimed as he burst through the door and trotted on twinkling legs to the group standing in the center of the room. "*¡Explícame acerca del Yanqui! ¿Por qué no lo capturaron?*"

With a shrug the Apache called Stenache looked at Eusebio, the expression on his face indicating that he expected the latter to do the explaining.

"*Será como esto, Don Pino,*" Eusebio replied. "*El Yanqui nos ha vi, y antes de alcanzarlo, galopó a la senda y fuera.*"

With difficulty Foxx kept from grinning when he heard the explanation Don Pino had demanded. He could visualize the feisty little Pepper showing the heels of his horse to pursuit as he galloped up the path out of the canyon.

"*¿Por qué no corricron detrás de él tonto?*" Pino demanded. "*¿Tienen buenos caballos, no?*"

"*Sí, Don Pino,*" Eusebio replied. "*Solamente obedecemos sus órdenes que nunca nos vayamos del valle antes de la noche.*"

"*¡Qué tonteria!*" Pino yelled, his temper flaring up because his own orders to stay in the canyon until dark had been taken too literally. "*¿Por esto permitieron al Yanqui escaparse?*"

"*Don Pino, sus órdenes—*" Stenache began.

"*¡Cállate, estúpido!*" Pino snapped. "*¡Un guerrero de Mangas Coloradas me dice esto! ¿No te enseñó nada mi padre?*"

Foxx's ears pricked up at the mention of the Apache chief who had left a trail of depredation across the southern part of Arizona Territory. Mangas Coloradas—Red Sleeves—had been killed ten years or more ago, as nearly as Foxx could remember, and now it appeared that his son—if Pino was indeed that—had picked up the torch of devastation where Mangas had dropped it. Suddenly the activities of the night riders began to fall into a pattern in Foxx's mind, but he had no time to search for the pattern's missing pieces, for Pino's companion began talking.

"*El Yanqui no estará tan lejos, Pino,*" the big man

said. *"Despácha todos nuestros guerreros para rastrearlo."*

Pino's rage had subsided. He nodded his agreement with the big man's suggestion that the entire gang be sent to follow Pepper's trail, and said, *"Bueno, Otero."* Turning to Alvarez, he went on, *"Encárgate, Alvarez. ¡Inmediatamente! ¡Y no vuelven sin el Yanqui!"*

There was a bustle of activity as the men began moving toward the stairway. Foxx tried to think of a way to turn the diversion of their attention to his own advantage, but before he had a chance to do more than consider the possibilities, the big man called Otero was at his side, his hamlike hand clamped on Foxx's biceps.

"You will not need this, now I have your gun," he said, taking off Foxx's gunbelt and hanging it over a chair back. "Now, you will come with us, Foxx. Pino has matters he wishes to discuss with you."

"We must go on with our discussion of the night before last, Foxx," Pino said. "You did not listen well to the offer I have made you then. Here in my headquarters it might be that you will consider more careful what I have said before."

When Pino switched from Spanish to English, Foxx's surprise was so complete that he forgot to keep his face expressionless for the small man's voice underwent a complete transformation: The high-pitched, almost shrill tone which marked his speech when he was talking in Spanish vanished, and the timbre of his voice deepened. At that moment Foxx recognized him as the unseen man with whom he'd had such a long conversation when he and Pepper were camped on the bank of the Bill Williams River two nights earlier.

Pino saw the recognition in Foxx's eyes and nodded. "Ah," he said, "I see that you are remembering our conversation."

"It ain't likely that I'd forget it," Foxx replied. "It wasn't all that long ago."

"And I am sure that you recognized Alvarez, too?" Pino shook his head with mock sadness. "He watched you kill his best friend in a saloon in La Paz. You should walk with care when you are near Alvarez, Foxx. He has it in his mind to kill you."

"Oh, Alvarez told me that hisself awhile ago," Foxx said. "I won't lose too much sleep worrying about him, though."

"Perhaps you do not have too much time left to worry," Pino suggested. "But it is possible that I can help you escape from Alvarez, if you listen to me with more attention than you did before." He turned to Otero. *"Vámonos a la sala para hablar de esto. Vete, Otero."*

Otero was still holding Foxx's arm. He tightened the grip of his big hands, swung Foxx around to face the door leading to the adjoining room, and propelled him ahead, none too gently. Foxx made no effort to resist. He knew that if he did put up a fight against a man of Otero's size and strength, he would lose more than the fight. He would sacrifice that intangible dignity the Indians called "face" and weaken what little bargaining power he had. He marched coolly ahead of Otero into the adjoining room.

Passing through the door was like going from a cottage to a palace. The second room took in the balance of that floor of the huge building, as closely as Foxx could tell. Its furniture and appointments were luxurious. Small gilded tables stood beside matching chairs, and silk-upholstered sofas stood against the walls, alternating with cabinets and chests. Larger veneered tables stood centered in each end of the huge room. Gilt-framed paintings—portraits, hunting scenes, rural vistas—hung on the walls. A crystal chandelier dropped from the high ceiling. Magnificent rugs covered the floor.

In spite of the luxury Foxx sensed something disharmonious about the room. Looking more closely, he saw what was wrong. The upholstery of the furniture was frayed, the gilt of the frames was chipped and rubbed. The polish of the tables was dusty, too, and on close inspection Foxx could see the nicks and scratches that marred the rich wood. The chandelier glistened in spite of a layer of grime that coated its crystal drops. The rugs were threadbare.

"This is a right fancy place you got here," Foxx remarked casually to Pino as Otero guided him to an armchair and pushed him down to its seat. "Must've been built quite awhile ago, the way it looks to me."

"It was built by the family of my mother," Pino told him. "Her people abandoned it when you Yanquis pushed them from the land. It stood deserted for many years before my father learned of it. When your soldiers pressed him too closely, he used it as a secret refuge, and never did they find it."

Foxx cudgeled his brain for dates, never his strong point in the small amount of schooling he'd had. He did remember two key dates. Arizona came under U.S. sovereignty after the Mexican War of 1846, and many of the few original colonists from Spain and Mexico who'd settled north of the Gila River had returned to Mexico after that. Most of those who had remained gave up and went back to the land from which their ancestors had come when the Gadsden Purchase in 1855 pushed the Arizona-Mexico border almost two hundred miles further south of the Gila. But searching his memory for dates also stirred Foxx's curiosity.

"Didn't I hear you saying something about Mangas Coloradas a minute ago?" he asked Pino.

"You have heard the name before, then?" Pina asked proudly.

"Why, sure. I don't guess there's many folks that hasn't. From what I heard about him, he was a pretty good fighting man."

For the first time, Pino's hostile attitude changed. His voice puzzled, he said, "I find this strange, Foxx. You do not speak of Mangas Coloradas as others do. You sound as though you might almost understand that he fought for the homeland of his tribe. For doing what any brave man would do, most of your people call him a murdering savage."

Foxx chose his words carefully when he replied. "Why, I always figured that from the way he looked at things he was fighting in a war. And I ain't heard of no wars yet where folks didn't get killed."

Pino's eyes brightened. "Yes. Yes, it was a war Mangas Coloradas fought. But he did not die in battle. I am the son of Mangas Coloradas, Foxx! I speak only the truth about him!"

"Well, you ain't heard me saying you're a liar, Pino."

"Here." Pino fumbled at the fawn-colored gloves he had on. "I will show you what your soldiers did to me when I was but a child too small to fight." He finally succeeded in getting one glove off and quickly tore away the other. "Only because I am of Mangas Coloradas the son, they cripple me!"

Pino extended his hands. They looked like the stumps of trees dragged by force from the earth, some roots broken and others left intact. Pino's fingers had been chopped off, not evenly, but some at the palm, others at the middle joint, and his thumbs had been amputated. Only the little fingers on each hand had been left whole.

"You're telling me that U.S. soldiers done this?" Foxx asked incredulously.

"This, too, is true!" Pino exclaimed. "But it is nothing to what they did to my father. After they shot him, they cut his head off from his body and boiled from it the flesh! Then they sent it to be stared at by any who wished to look!"

"Now, I never heard about anything like that," Foxx said.

Pino did not seem to hear him. He ignored Foxx's interruption and went on, "How can the spirit of Mangas Coloradas rest while his body remains apart, Foxx? No, it must be brought together! To do this, I am making my father's vision of the Apacheria a real thing!"

"¡Pino!" Otero said sharply. "¡No es la hora de discutir tu sueño! ¡Tenemos negocios más importantes con este hombre!"

"Sí, Otero, ya lo sé. Pero es importante también mi sueño."

"Pues quédate con tu sueño," Otero admonished the younger man. *"Si tenemos buen éxito con Foxx, después hablamos de esta cosa."*

Pino was too full of his plans to be stopped. He dismissed Otero's warning with a flick of one mutilated hand and went on, "It was the dream of my father to drive the whites from what you call the Gadsden lands, and in it restore the Apacheria."

"That'd be a pretty big job, Pino." Foxx frowned. "And I don't see why you'd be helping any by trying to stop the C&K from building a railroad way north of the Gila River like we're trying to do. Why, the Gila's two hundred miles or more south of here."

"Ah, but railroads bring your people from the East, and if they once arrive in numbers, they will push into the Apacheria!"

"Pino!" Otero broke in, his voice sharper and angrier than before. *"¡Con eso basta! ¡Hablamos ahorita solamente de hechos positivos! ¿Estamos de acuerdo?"*

"Bueno, Otero." Pino sighed. *"Más tarde, será como dices."* He turned back to Foxx. "Otero is right, we must first talk of what has not been finished between us, Foxx. I have made you the offer. You will be paid well for your help. This you have thought of, no?"

"Oh, I've thought about it, Pino," Foxx replied. "And I still say I don't aim to make no kind of deal with you."

"Perhaps it is that Pino has not explain all," Otero suggested. "Perhaps it is that he has not tell you what will your fate be if you refuse. Come with us, Foxx. There is a thing that you must see."

Without waiting for Foxx to reply, Otero clamped his arm in another viselike grip and led him to one of the large, ornate chests that stood at one side of the room. He released his grip and took a large key from the pocket of his trousers. Unlocking the chest, he lifted the lid. A nauseating odor flowed from the chest. It reminded Foxx of the stomach-wrenching smell that hung over a Comanche camp a week or so after the Kotsotekas had staged a successful buffalo hunt, a penetrating fetidness which combined the aromas of musty fur and soured blood, overlaid with the stench of rotting flesh.

Neither Pino or Otero seemed to notice the foul smell, and Foxx did not show that it bothered him. Otero reached into the chest and pulled out a human scalp. The grisly trophy had been badly scraped, and bits of corrupting flesh hung from its edges. He dangled the scalp in front of Foxx's face. Foxx gazed at it impassively.

"Do you not recognize this, Foxx?" the big man asked.

"Sure. I seen scalps before now."

"It is not only the scalp I speak of," Otero said. "Surely you can say from the head of who it came?"

Foxx shook his head. "No. Except he was a white man."

Pino giggled, a high, thin boyish pulsing deep in his throat. "It is from one of the men you have sent here! Do you not know the scalps of your own people, then?"

"I know their faces," Foxx replied coolly, "not their hair, Pino."

"There are many more in here," Otero said. "Look well into our treasure chest!"

He tightened his grip on Foxx's arm and pulled him forward, using his great strength to force Foxx to lean over the chest. Foxx tightened his throat to keep from gagging. Close as he was now to the chest, the stench from the many scalps was even stronger.

His face impassive, Foxx gazed at the gruesome display. He could see only the top layer of scalps, a mixture of brown and blond and black hair anchored in caps of dead skin and flesh. Foxx guessed there must be twenty to thirty of the trophies in the chest. He said nothing and stayed motionless, not resisting, until Otero released his arm and stepped back.

Foxx needed to get the smell of corruption out of his lungs. He said, "I don't guess you'd object if I light up a cigar?"

Pino gave permission with a quick gesture and watched as Foxx lighted a twisted stogie and exhaled a cloud of smoke.

"Well?" Pino asked impatiently. "What do you think of our treasure?"

"It don't impress me all that much, Pino. It's just a mess of stinking hair." The sharp fumes of the cigar helped to dispel the odor of the scalps but could not mask it completely. Foxx saw Pino and Otero watching him, their faces puzzled. He went on calmly, "No, that ain't the kind of treasure I got much use for."

"Still he does not understand," Pino said to the big man. "Tell him, Otero."

"They are money, these scalps," Otero explained. He saw the look of questioning surprise that passed over Foxx's face and went on, "Oh, no! We do not for our pleasure the scalps take. Each one is to us worth much money."

"We have learn much from your people," Pino added. "When they came first to the Apacheria, they paid well to anyone who brought them scalps of Apaches. It was before I remember, but my people do not forget such things! Now, for each scalp from a worker on your railroad, we are paid five hundred of your silver dollars."

"That's what your gang really works at, then?" Foxx asked. "Just collecting scalps of people that work for the C&K?"

"*Seguro,*" Otero replied. "Your people owe ours a debt of many more scalps than we take! We who are of Apache blood, me, Chato, Stenache, Guevavi, Alvarez, Pino, we would take them even if we do not get paid. If we get paid, it is better than take them for no money, yes?"

"Not in my book, it ain't."

Foxx wondered just how many scalps in the chest had been taken from the bodies of C&K workers. He recalled Riley's remark that railroaders were a footloose lot, and remembered that even in San Francisco and Oakland men walked off their jobs every day without telling their foremen they were quitting, and he imagined that even more men left the outlying division yards and the railhead construction camps in the same fashion. Quitting without notice was so common on all railroads that when a man did not show up after a two-day absence, the paymaster simply scratched his name off the time sheet and notified the gang foreman that the missing man had quit, and the foreman hired a new worker.

Then Foxx's mind returned to the still-unanswered question of who was paying for the scalps. Keeping his voice casual, he asked, "Who pays you all that money you get for them scalps, Pino?"

"This is not for you to know!" Otero put in quickly, before Pino could answer. "But something else I will tell you, Foxx. For such time as the railroad tracks do not cross the Santa Maria River, each scalp to us is worth much money. Now, Foxx, do you not wish to share our fortune?"

"Well?" Pino asked when Foxx said nothing. "What do you say now to our offer?"

"Just what I said all along. No deal, Pino."

"Think well, Foxx!" Otero warned. "Think well of how much the scalp of such an important man like you is worth to us. For it we will not get only five hundred dollars. No, for your scalp we will get a thousand! Do you wish your scalp to join the others in our treasure chest?"

CHAPTER 11

"That's a fool question to ask a man, Otero," Foxx said calmly. "It ain't worth wasting my breath answering it."

Otero raised Foxx's Smith & Wesson and leveled it. Foxx ignored the threat but cudgeled his mind trying to work out a way to get to the Colt Cloverleaf that still remained hidden in his boot top.

Pino said quickly, *"¡Quédate, Otero! ¡No te apresures! ¡Ya no lo mates a Foxx! ¡No ha visto ya mamá! Se enojadará si olvidamos su gusto."*

To Foxx, Pino's remarks to Otero made no sense. He suppressed a frown as he tried to figure out what connection there was between Pino's mother and the command he'd given Otero not to shoot him until later.

Otero said, *"Lo siento, Pinito. He olvidado."* He smiled grimly. *"Tal vez entretanto la señora convencerá a Foxx a hacer nuestra."*

"Es posible." Pino nodded. He said to Foxx, "We will give you some time to think once more. Do not expect for us to be so generous again, though." Turning back to Otero, he went on, *"Pues, toma Foxx a la torre y prepárate. Voy y digo a mamá que esta listo."*

Otero nodded and closed the chest, but the odor of the scalps still hung heavily in the air. He said to Foxx, "We are to go now." He waved the muzzle of the S&W at a door in one corner of the big room. "That way."

Still mulling over the conversation between Pino and Otero, Foxx made his way out the door and down a flight of stairs. As he preceded Otero, Foxx realized that the stairway led to one of the castle's towers, which explained at least part of Pino's last instructions to Otero.

Foxx reached the bottom of the stairs and entered a square room with the high slit windows he'd noticed when first observing the castle from the canyon's rim. The shutters were closed, and the room was lighted only by thin slivers of fading daylight that crept in through the cracks of the shutters.

At first he thought that the room was totally unfurnished, but as his eyes adjusted to the twilight, he saw that it held two or three chairs, a small table, and an odd T-shaped piece of furniture that he could not identify. Foxx finally decided that it was a backless bench or work trestle of some kind; it stood only thigh-high, and as he studied the piece, he saw that it was fitted with straps and buckles at each end of its central section and the crossarms.

Otero indicated the bench with the muzzle of the

revolver. "You will lie down, Foxx. And do not foolish ideas get, or I will use this!"

Still wondering what was in store for him, Foxx lay down on the bench. Otero motioned for him to extend his arms along the crossbar, and Foxx again obeyed. He watched with mixed curiosity and worry as the big man secured his wrists with the straps at each end of the crossbar, then moved on to fasten Foxx's ankles with the straps at each side of the bench's bottom end.

Foxx was conscious of the danger that the giant might discover the Colt Cloverleaf in his boot while adjusting the straps, even though the bulge it made was almost invisible in the dim light of the shuttered tower room.

"You mind telling me what this is all about?" he asked, more to distract Otero's attention than because he felt the need to know.

Otero smiled smugly as he replied, "Soon enough you will find out. Enjoy yourself, Foxx. And think well of what Pino and I have told you will happen if you continue to be stubborn."

For a moment Otero stared at Foxx, as though waiting for him to ask again why he was being strapped to the bench or what was now in store for him. Foxx met the big man's eyes with his own unwavering gaze but remained stubbornly silent. When he saw that he was not going to get any further reaction, Otero shrugged and left the tower room.

In the complete silence that followed Otero's departure, Foxx lay in the deepening gloom until he was sure the giant was not going to return. Then he began tugging at the straps that held him to the bench. He tried each in turn, but there was no play in the leather tethers that were fastened around his wrists and ankles and held him immobilized. No matter how hard he strained, he found no way to rid himself of the straps. Otero had done his work very well indeed.

Tiring after repeated efforts, Foxx relaxed and began to turn over in his mind the possible reasons for this strange form of imprisonment. Despite some wild flights of imagination, he could find no answers.

He started thinking about Pepper, wondering whether he'd succeeded in escaping from the renegades or whether they had picked up his trail at the rim of the canyon. That train of thought led him nowhere, and after a second unsuccessful attempt at the straps, he began to reconsider his own predicament. The tower door swung open, and an oblong of light was thrown across the floor of the big square room.

Feet shuffled on the wooden floor. The light flickered, and in a moment a woman came into the room wearing a long, straight robe and carrying a tray on which a glass-chimneyed candlestick rested beside a tall bottle. Foxx got only a fleeting glimpse of her face, for as she entered she turned to close the door and bolt it.

She turned back and started to cross the room, giving Foxx a view of her face in profile, and for a moment he was unsure of what he saw. It was as though he was looking at a skull. From her brow to her chin her face curved in a single unbroken line. Foxx blinked and his eyes widened, then he understood. The woman across the room had no nose.

Paying no attention to Foxx, the woman went to the low table that stood near the foot of the bench and placed the tray on it. When she faced Foxx again, the light was behind her, but there was enough illumination in the room for him to see her clearly.

She wore her long blond hair loose, streaming down her back. Her forehead was a high oval, and her heavily rouged cheekbones protruded sharply from the elongated oval of her face. The prominent cheekbones emphasized her large dark eyes, open wide and glistening below the pencil-thin arches of her eyebrows. Two black holes showed where her nostrils should have been. Her mouth was a wide red gash above a small pointed chin.

For a moment she stared at Foxx in silence, then she said, *"Pinito me dice que cae bien."*

Foxx was still gazing at her with a look of incomprehension on his face. She mistook the reason for his puzzled stare.

"¿No sabe español?" she asked.

Foxx's only edge still remained his ability to understand most of what his captors were saying, and he had no intention of dulling that edge by admitting to any knowledge of their language, so he shook his head.

She tried again, her voice hopeful, *"Peut-être vous parlez français?"*

When Foxx shook his head a second time, the woman sighed and shrugged.

"Eh, bien. We will speak your barbaric English, then. But I always hope they will bring me a visitor I can talk with in my own tongue. What is your name, man? Pinito did not tell me."

Foxx was slow in replying. He'd recalled a half-forgotten remark made by one of the men downstairs, when he'd first been brought up from the stable, about a Frenchwoman being pleased. The reference had been a fleeting one, puzzling at the time, but now its significance came to him in a rush. He was sure by now that she must be descended from one of the French families that had come to Mexico after Napoleon III had made it virtually a colony of France. Then the woman spoke and broke his train of thought.

"You do speak English, don't you, man?" she asked.

"Oh. Sure. My name's Foxx."

She clapped her hands. *"Quelle blague! Le petit reynard!* But not *trop petit,* I hope. And you may call me Sylvie."

Foxx was still too surprised to say anything. Sylvie stepped to the table where she'd put the tray and picked up the bottle that stood beside the candle. She swayed slightly as she leaned to pick up the bottle, and Foxx realized for the first time that she must be more than a little drunk. Tilting the bottle to her lips, she swallowed twice, then held it out to Foxx.

"You would enjoy a small drink, no? To improve your strength? It is good cognac, you understand, brought from home long ago, when times were better." When Foxx neither accepted or refused, she went on, "Take a sip, now, to make Sylvie happy."

Foxx nodded, and she held the bottle while he drank. She put it back on the table and began fumbling at her throat, untying the neck cord of her robe. As she pulled at the tassels, she kept chattering in the fashion of one who spends much time alone and blossoms into extensive discourse when an audience is available.

"I have come to give you pleasure, Foxx. Much pleasure! Oh, you will return to me the pleasure, of course. I will make sure of that."

She let the robe fall from her shoulders. Foxx had not given any thought to Sylvie in terms of age, or in terms of anything but his own astonishment. Except for the few instants when she had held the cognac bottle for him to drink, he had seen her only at a distance, with the light at her back.

Now, looking at her naked body, he judged that she was in her late forties or early fifties. Her breasts had the relaxed sag that comes to women after they lose the upstanding tautness of youth and before their once-firm tissues shrivel to bags of wrinkled skin. Her abdomen was flat, and her buttocks too large for her slender hips. Her legs were thin; they rose like slender taperless columns to the wisp of her blond pubic hair, which was so pale that for a moment Foxx thought it had been shaved clean.

"Ah, you admire me, do you not, Foxx!" Sylvie said, turning coquettishly to display her nudity from all angles. "And you will not mind that I have no nose, eh?" She came close to the bench and began to stroke Foxx's groin as she went on, "My poor lost nose! It was removed many years ago by Pinito's father, when he caught me enjoying one of his young warriors. I did not know of that Apache way of punishment then, or I would not have been so careless."

While she talked, Sylvie bent over Foxx and started to unbutton his fly. She slid her hand into its opening and groped to find him, but Foxx was totally quiescent. Her hand wandering over his linen underwear, Sylvie continued to talk.

"But it is not a woman's nose that is important, eh, *petit reynard*? Nor a man's either, I suppose. But why do I not find the most important part of a man on you, Foxx? Surely Pinito would not send me an incomplete man!"

With a small snort of displeasure she unbuckled Foxx's belt, pulled his trousers down around his thighs, and unbuttoned the underwear that had been foiling her efforts. As she found the roll of flesh that she'd been seeking and closed her hand around its softness, Sylvie went back to her interrupted discourse. As people tend to do in moments of distraction, she dropped now and then into her native tongue.

"Oh, *mais oui*, you are complete, Foxx! *C'est très bien. Une abondance de biens ne nuit pas.* Ah, but you are unready! And Sylvie needs you at once!"

She threw one leg across Foxx's hips to straddle him and brought his tip up between her thighs. Slowly and gently she began rubbing him against her. Foxx had no need to warn himself that he must not be affected by the soft, warm moisture of Sylvie's inner lips. His body simply failed to respond.

After she had been caressing herself with Foxx's limp flesh for several moments, Sylvie said unhappily, "What is wrong with you, Foxx? *Tu ne reponds pas!*"

She increased the pressure with which she was rubbing and stopped briefly from time to time to try to bury Foxx's softness within her, but each time she failed.

"*Qu'est-ce qu'il a?*" she muttered, more to herself than to Foxx. "*Il est maladif!*"

Sylvie changed her position. Moving as though Foxx did not exist except as an object for her use, she sat on his hips, her legs spread. Foxx could not see what she was doing, but when he felt her fingers seeking him again and then felt her begin rubbing his tip on her wetness, he understood. He lay quietly, not enjoying, not protesting, seeing the beginning of a plan that might get him free, devoting his attention to working out the details.

While Foxx thought, Sylvie massaged herself with a quiet, intense concentration. Her body began to shake, gently at first, then faster, as she increased the tempo of her rubbing, until she shook with quick convulsions and sighed lingeringly while holding him pressed to her with one hand.

"*C'est mieux.*" She sighed abstractedly.

She stepped to the floor, still ignoring Foxx's presence, and went to the table to drink again. This time she did not offer Foxx the bottle.

"*Qu'est-ce—*" she began, looking down at him, then suddenly remembered that he could not understand her. She shook her head and started over. "What is wrong, Foxx? Is it that you are a lover of boys, who does not like women?"

"Oh, it ain't that. I just don't seem to do a woman no good when I'm all tied up this way," he replied.

Sylvie glanced at the straps that held Foxx captive, and for a moment he thought she was going to unbuckle them. Then she shook her head determinedly.

"No, no, Sylvie does not make twice the same mistake," she said. "I know better than to release you,

Foxx. Once I did this for some man, and for a month Pinito refused to bring me another. Only when I had promised him that nevermore would I be so foolish did I have visitors again."

"I'm afraid I can't do you no good, then, Sylvie," Foxx told her, forcing a note of regret into his voice.

Sylvie drank again and put the bottle down. She came back to the bench, and now she was smiling. *"N'importe,"* she said. *"Je m'en occupe."*

Dropping to her knees, Sylvie lifted Foxx's limp shaft and began to caress it again. She bent closer to Foxx, holding him erect with her hands. He felt Sylvie's warm breath on him, and then the tip of her tongue touched him softly, experimentally. Foxx lay with the stillness of a man frozen, willing himself now not to respond to the warmth that engulfed him as Sylvie drew him into her mouth. Her clinging lips moved up and down, and her tongue rasped around him with the agility of a serpent's twining as she drew him in even more deeply.

Foxx's mind was unable to subdue his flesh. He felt himself swelling, and as Sylvie prolonged her skillful caresses, now teasing him with flicks of her tongue, now taking him in so deeply that the hot cavern of her mouth was totally filled, Foxx's swelling became a rock-hard erection.

Sylvie continued to pluck at his erection with her wet, writhing lips until she was satisfied that she'd achieved her objective. Foxx felt the cool air sweep over him for a moment, then Sylvie had thrown her leg over him to straddle him again. She raised herself to position Foxx's hard, ruddy shaft and let herself fall down on him. Small throaty sighs of pleasure burst from her lips as she felt Foxx inside her. She pushed herself up and let her weight down a second time, more deliberately, prolonging his entry, until her thighs settled on his hips. She bent her knees, trying to allow him to go deeper.

"*Cela me va.*" She sighed. "*C'est bien, c'est marveilleux!*"

For a few moments Sylvie crouched over Foxx, squirming from side to side, until her excitement mounted and she could stay still no longer.

"*Cela me va!*" she cried, her voice trembling, then she lifted herself and dropped back. "*Allez, Foxx! Allez-y!*"

Foxx tried to will himself into softness again when Sylvie began rocking her body back and forth over him, but he'd been aroused too far. He lay motionless, feeling her push herself up and drop back down with her full weight in a free fall that sent Foxx into her utmost depths. Then she abandoned the slow, deep rise and fall that brought the deepest penetration. Stretching out full length, she began a slow rotation of her hips as she lowered and raised her buttocks. She sought Foxx's lips, but he turned his head away, and Sylvie contented herself with nibbling and licking his throat.

"*Vite, Foxx, vite!*" she commanded, her forehead wrinkling into a frown that could have expressed either anger or passion.

Foxx did not answer or move. He let her bounce and squirm as she wished, until she was once again rising and falling on him in a mad fury. He felt her falter after she'd kept up the furious pace a short while, and then fall forward on him, her body wracked with spasmodic shudders which went on and on until he thought they would never end. Finally Sylvie's tense muscles grew slack and she lay on him full length, without moving.

Sylvie's quick, shallow breathing became more regular as time ticked away. She stirred and moved her hips experimentally. She said, "Foxx? You are still stiff and big. Did you feel nothing?"

"I told you, I ain't much good when I'm tied down."

"No, Foxx! I will not free you! But unless you share my feeling, I am not satisfied! Now we will start again, before you shrink, and I will show you that you can do what you say you cannot."

Foxx lost count of the number of times Sylvie tried to bring him to climax, but she seemed to be insatiable when aroused as she was by her compulsion to do so. Each time Foxx began to soften, she teased him back to an erection with lips and tongue before mounting him again and rocking to complete her own spasm, then refreshed by a swallow or two of cognac, returned to the bench to try again. The candle on the table had burned to a stub little more than an inch long, and the cognac bottle was nearly empty when Foxx judged the time had come to make another effort.

"Look here, Sylvie," he said. "I'd like to do what you want me to, but it ain't going to happen as long as I'm laying on my back this way, with you doing all the humping up on top. I got to be free so I can hump you. That's the only way I'm any good."

Sylvie gazed at Foxx, still standing firmly erect in spite of her efforts. She sighed wistfully. "You are sure?" she asked. Her words were blurred, her voice uncertain.

"I'm sure. Ain't I been telling you the same thing since you first started out?"

"*Oui, c'est vrai.*"

She hesitated momentarily, then went to the end of the bench and loosened the straps that held Foxx's feet. She hesitated longer before freeing his wrists, and though Foxx wanted to tell her to hurry, he sensed that it would be a mistake. He waited until she'd removed the last strap, then stood up. Without thinking, he took a step forward and almost fell as his dangling trousers caught his feet.

Regaining his balance, Foxx bent to pull the trousers up, but Sylvie was at his side instantly. He was surprised when he saw how short she was. When he'd been lying down looking up at her, she had seemed to tower over her. Now, as she came up to him, her bare breasts were only inches above his waist.

"Hurry now, Foxx!" she said impatiently. She rubbed against him, pulling at his erection, trying to bring it down to her thighs. She was not tall enough. Even when she stood on tiptoe, she could not lift her body high enough to take him in. She whirled around, her back to Foxx. Bending over, she reached between her outspread legs and tucked him into her.

"Now, Foxx!" she urged. "You are free! Do not stop until I feel your spurting juices fill me!"

To keep her from raising a protesting shout that might have aroused the castle, Foxx thrust distractedly. He knew that most of the night was gone, and that he must make the most of his freedom at once, but the thought of killing or even badly hurting the defenseless Sylvie repelled him. Finally he took the gentlest way he knew of silencing her. Without interrupting his halfhearted stroking, he wrapped his hand around her mouth, covering it and the holes where her nose had been. Absorbed in the sensations she so enjoyed, Sylvie did not realize at first what Foxx intended. When she did, she began to struggle, but her strength was puny compared to Foxx's. Her efforts to free herself grew weaker, and finally, the air in her lungs exhausted, she slumped, unconscious.

Lowering Sylvie's limp form to the floor, Foxx belted up his trousers, then tore a strip of cloth from Sylvie's robe with which to bind and gag her. She regained consciousness while he was knotting the gag, and though she could not speak, her eyes accused him. Foxx turned his back and began adjusting his clothing so that he could move freely. Then he slid the Colt Cloverleaf from his boot top and blew out the guttering candle before opening the door and starting silently up the stairs.

After he'd covered half the distance to the big main room above, Foxx stopped to look and listen. The windows of the vast chamber had not been shuttered, and he saw that the muted gray of false dawn was already stealing across the wall of the canyon visible from the window nearest the stairs. Belatedly Foxx realized that there was a lighted lamp standing on a table near one of the divans. The back of the divan was toward the stairs, but from the size of the booted feet that protruded beyond the arm of the sofa, Foxx deduced that the man sleeping there was the giant Otero.

Stepping as lightly as he knew how, Foxx made his way across the room. The carpets helped muffle his careful progress. He saw his own Smith & Wesson on the table beside the lamp as he got closer to the sofa and the sleeping man, and his hand itched to reach for it, the Cloverleaf Colt he held weighed too little to be effective as a club.

Thinking of the two weapons reminded Foxx that the Cloverleaf was still in its carrying mode. He thumbed the hammer back to bring a cylinder into position. Slight as was the noise made by the revolver's mechanism, it roused the sleeping man.

Otero sat up, turned, and saw Foxx. He reached for the S&W on the table, but Foxx's finger was already on the trigger of the Cloverleaf. He squeezed off the shot, and the heavy .41 slug spurting from the revolver's inch-long barrel smashed into the back of Otero's head just as the giant's groping hand touched the Smith & Wesson.

CHAPTER 12

Foxx moved swiftly now, knowing that from the instant he'd triggered the Colt Cloverleaf, the shot's explosion banished any reason for stealth. He did not know the layout of the rest of the huge house, or how many people might be in it, but he was certain that someone would be after him at once. As soon as he'd picked up the S&W and tucked it into his waistband, he ran for the narrow room that led to the stairs leading to the stables.

Bootheels clattering on the tile floor of the narrow room where he'd first been taken, he made for the door of the stairway. He had almost reached it when he realized that he'd just seen his own gunbelt and holster hanging on the back of one of the chairs, where Alvarez had put it earlier. He spent a few valuable moments going back the three or four steps necessary to retrieve the belt and headed for the stairway, buckling on the gunbelt as he ran down the stairs to the stables.

A lantern still burned in the cavernous area, though the dawn light was flowing through the door that led outside. Foxx breathed more easily when he saw that most of the stalls were vacant, for that made possible two welcome deductions. The first was that Alvarez and the rest of the renegade gang were still out looking for Pepper. The second was that if the pursuers hadn't returned by this time, they'd lost Pepper's trail in the darkness and were just now resuming their pursuit.

Given any luck, Foxx was sure that he could trail the gang and, by pushing hard, might overtake Alvarez and his men, or at least be close enough to take a hand in a showdown when they finally closed in on Pepper.

Moving hurriedly between the lines of stalls, Foxx found the one into which his horse had been put. By all the evidence he saw, the horse had been shoved hurriedly into the nearest stall when Alvarez had ordered his men to pursue Pepper.

Whoever was attending to the stable chores had apparently been commanded by Alvarez to drop everything and join in the chase, for Foxx's horse was still saddled. Even the Winchester had been replaced in the saddle scabbard. Nor had his saddlebags been searched, Foxx discovered when he felt in them; his gear was just as he'd packed it. He took out a fresh bundle of stogies, broke the seal, and lighted one of the short, twisted cigars while he looked for the harness gear.

He found the bit, bridle, and reins lying in a

tangled heap on the floor of the next stall, and from that point it was a job of only two or three minutes to get the horse ready to travel. Foxx mounted and rode out the open door just as he heard the faint sound of voices calling back and forth in the rooms above him. Heading around the building, he prodded the horse with his bootheels and turned it toward the foot of the path that led out of the canyon.

Fresh, fed, and rested, the horse trotted up the cutback path in much less time than it had taken to descend it the previous day. Foxx kept looking down into the canyon for signs of pursuit but saw none until he'd reached the rim. Then two riders came galloping around the corner of the castle.

Even at that distance Foxx recognized one of them as Pino. He frowned as he studied the second rider, who seemed even smaller than Pino. The riders had not yet looked up and seen him, and Foxx did not wait for a closer look at them. He put the apparent size of the second pursuer down to an optical illusion created by the angle, and spurred his horse away from the canyon rim, across the arid mesa.

Foxx had enough of a start on the pair just setting out after him to relieve him of worrying about them overtaking him soon, but still he pushed his mount as fast as he dared. The rising sun was low and quartering his back, throwing the surface of the mesa into sharp relief and making the fresh tracks of Pepper's pursuers stand out. He had no difficulty in following the trail of the renegades who had been sent out by Pino to bring Pepper back to the castle. In making his escape the feisty little Texan had simply ridden in a straight line toward the Bill Williams River at the fastest pace to which he could urge his horse.

Foxx could not always distinguish the prints of Pepper's mount from those of his pursuers, but occasionally the two trails diverged for short distances and provided him with the assurance that the tracks he followed were the right ones. Lack of speed seemed to be the gang's main problem; as Foxx read their hoofprints, they had not maintained as fast a pace as he was setting himself, and they had stopped as soon as the fading daylight hid Pepper's tracks.

When Foxx reached the edge of the mesa, where Alvarez and his men had stopped for the night, the morning was still young. They had made a dry camp, and Foxx stopped only long enough to investigate the dung dropped by their horses. Its condition indicated that the renegades were not more than two or three hours ahead of him.

Until his stop at the gang's camp Foxx had not seen the pair that was chasing him. He glimpsed them as he left the campsite, dark figures on the endless horizon, visible not as individuals but as moving shapes seen in silhouette through the heat haze that was just beginning to shimmer in the clear air. The distance was too great for him to try to identify Pino's companion; indeed, through the roiling air it was impossible even to tell which of the riders was Pino.

By pressing his horse hard across the long upslope of broken country that lay between the mesa and the Bill Williams River, Foxx got to the stream shortly before noon. He pulled up fifty yards from the bank and lighted a stogie while he let the horse breathe and cool off before walking it to the stream to drink.

He could see the trail on the other side of the river, and the manure piles left by the renegades' horses told him he was closing the gap fast; the gang now had a lead of less than an hour on him. Smiling confidently, he toed the horse to the water's edge, stopped to let it drink sparingly, then started to ford the stream.

He was halfway across when the horse stumbled as a loose rock turned under its hoof. Foxx managed to stay in the saddle when the animal broke stride and almost went down, but the horse was trembling nervously. He let it stand in midstream for a few minutes until its trembling subsided, but it moved with a halting limp when he toed it forward again to complete the river crossing.

Foxx let the horse pick its way across the remainder of the ford, pulled up, and dismounted. The horse stood with its near front foot held off the ground. Foxx saw what was wrong as soon as he looked at the animal's hoof, and began to swear silently at the liveryman at Hell on Wheels for failing to take better care of his stock.

At some time during the hard riding he'd been doing, the badly worn shoe on the front hoof had begun dropping its nails. The next-to-last nail had probably come out when the animal crossed the loose stones at the start of the river crossing. Now the shoe was held by a single nail, and the iron crescent had twisted on the hoof.

Dropping to his knees, Foxx worked at the shoe, trying to pull it free. He'd almost succeeded when the badly worn metal of the thinned shoe snapped at the nail. The shoe came away in two pieces, leaving a half-inch of the nail protruding from the hoof. Rid of the twisted shoe, the horse put its hoof down but lifted it with a whinny of protest when the stub of the nail caused the hoof to twist unevenly.

Foxx dropped the pieces of the shoe and settled back on his heels while he studied the problem. He knew the nail had to come out, but he had no tool with which to pull it out of the horny hoof in which it was imbedded. He lifted the hoof, took the nail in his fingers, and tugged, but it did not budge. Lowering the hoof again, Foxx lighted a fresh stogie and racked his brain for a way to remove the crippling bit of metal.

His jaw set in anger, Foxx took out his pocketknife and began to whittle away the hoof in line with the headless nail. The horny layers that made up the hoof were tough, and after a short time the blade of Foxx's knife grew dull. He persevered, shaving away the tough, grainy horn until he could see the nail's shaft through the thin layer that still covered it. He grasped the protruding stub again, to try to pull it through the shell, and had just felt the nail beginning to break free when he heard hoofbeats coming along the south bank of the river.

A hump in the uneven terrain still hid the approaching riders from Foxx, but his ears told him there were two of them, and he was certain they could only be Pino and his companion. He looked around for a place to hide, but there was none. At the beginning of the Hualapai foothills there was no vegetation except a few thin stalks of ocotillo and an occasional patch of low salt cedar growing along the bank. Even if the closest of these clumps had been near enough for Foxx to reach with his crippled mount, their growth was too stunted and sparse to hide a horse or a man.

By now the rhythmic thumping of hoofbeats was getting very close. Foxx took the only course that occurred to him. To keep his horse from bolting and possibly injuring its hoof, he slid the reins over its head and wrapped them loosely around his thigh. He drew his S&W. Then he stretched out facedown, his right elbow bent into a vee, the gun ready in his hand but concealed under his left shoulder. He dropped his head to the ground and waited for the approaching riders to see him.

To Foxx it seemed that an eternity passed before they got to the spot where he was lying. His ears told him that the pair did not ride side by side; the hoofbeats of one of the horses was much louder than those of the other. One of them, he decided, must have stayed on the far bank of the river while the other crossed the stream as they searched for the place where he had crossed. If his horse hadn't been hurt, he would be across the river by now. Then the hoofbeats stopped, and Pino's voice, raised in a shout, reached his ears.

"*¡Owzó el río aquí! ¿Hay huellas en el otro lado?*" Pino called to his companion.

"*Si, hermanito,*" came the reply

Foxx frowned. The voice that replied was that of a woman. It was also a voice which Foxx recognized. The woman riding with Pino was Lita, whom he'd last seen leaving his room at the Arizona House in

Hell on Wheels, and from the reply she'd just made to Pino's question, he concluded that she was Pino's sister.

"*Hay un—*" Lita continued, then she paused for a moment and with her excitement evident in her tones, called, "*¡Mira, Pinito! ¡Ahora tenemos a Foxx! ¡Echado de su caballo! ¡Está inconsciente o tal vez muerto, no sé cuál!*"

"*Lo veolo mismo,*" Pino called back. "*Un momento, Lita. Voy a tu lado.*"

Over the sound of Pino's voice, followed by the splashes of his horse entering the river, Foxx heard the slow hoofbeats of Lita's mount draw closer and stop beside him. There was the thump of her boots hitting the ground as she dismounted, and then below the brim of his hat he saw the toes of her boots, inches from his face.

Foxx decided there was no point in waiting any longer to act. He uncoiled in a single swift movement that brought him to his feet, facing Lita, inches away from her. She stared at him, too surprised to move. Foxx grabbed her wrist and whirled her around, pulling her right arm down to imprison her left as he jerked her to him, her back against his chest. Lita struggled for a moment, but when she found that she could not break the grip of his strong hand, she subsided.

Foxx raised the S&W in his right hand to cover Pino, who had reached the middle of the river. "Stop right there, Pino!" he called. "And don't move your hands off of them reins!"

Pino hesitated, but Lita switched to English so that

Foxx would understand and cried, "Do as Foxx orders, Pino! If you don't, he'll kill you!"

For a moment Foxx thought that Pino was going to keep coming ahead in spite of Lita's command to stop. He leveled the pistol's muzzle to reinforce her words.

"Don't be a fool, Pinito!" Lita called. "You know you can't handle a gun! Obey Foxx, quickly!"

Reluctantly Pino nodded. He reined in, stopping in midstream, and stared with hot, angry eyes at Foxx, who held Lita in front of him.

Foxx was trying to think of something he could use to tie Lita, to free his hands so that he could deal with Pino. He looked at her, the first chance he'd had to do so since she had dismounted. She was wearing a charro jacket, a duplicate of the ornate gold-embroidered one that Pino wore, with a dark blouse under the jacket. Instead of the flared pants that usually went with the charro costume, Lita had on a divided riding skirt and calf-high boots. Her hat was a wide-brimmed Stetson of the same light-tan hue of the jacket and skirt. Her glistening black hair was braided, and the braids were looped in a figure-eight knot low on the nape of her neck. She stared back at Foxx defiantly.

Seeing no article of Lita's clothing that he could use to tie her with, Foxx looked elsewhere. His eyes caught the glint of bright metal on her ornate saddle, with its silver conchas and decorative strips of rawhide. Seeing the long strings of rawhide, Foxx realized that they would solve his problem.

"We're going to step over to your horse real slow, Lita," he told her. "And don't get no ideas about bust-ing loose. I ain't got much use for that brother of yours, and I'd about as soon shoot him as look at him."

Lita nodded sullenly. Foxx took a step toward her horse, pushing her ahead of him. Suddenly Lita became a snarling, spitting wildcat. She twisted against Foxx's arm, letting the full weight of her body sag against him. Foxx was forced to take his gun off Pino as he swung his right arm to regain his balance.

"*¡Cabalga rápidamente, Pino!*" Lita shouted. "*¡Anda! ¡Halla a los Apaches y vuelve pronto!*"

Pino turned his horse and started back across the river. Foxx was still trying to maintain his hold on Lita. She was twisting her lithe body, throwing herself forward, back, and from side to side. Foxx was constantly off-balance as he supported her dead weight with one arm while he tried to raise his revolver for a shot at the retreating Pino.

Lita began kicking backward, trying to hit Foxx's shins with her booted heels, and Foxx had to dance clumsily to avoid her flailing feet. He could not brace himself firmly enough to lift her off the ground without toppling down himself.

Pino reached the far bank, and Foxx fired twice, knowing they were desperation shots. The slugs went wide and did nothing except spatter up spurts of dust beside the hooves of Pino's horse. Then Pino was out of range, bending low in his saddle, galloping toward the castle.

As soon as Lita saw that Pino had escaped safely, she quit struggling. She twisted her head and snarled, "So now you have me, Foxx, but not for long! Pino will soon be back, and then we will see how long you can keep me!"

"Pino's got a ways to ride, and then he's got to ride back," Foxx reminded her. "By the time he gets back here with them Apaches you told him to find, we'll have so much of a lead that they never will catch up."

"You understood what I told him?" she asked, her eyes widening in surprise. "I did not know you spoke Spanish!"

"Well, I don't talk your lingo, Lita. But when you commenced yelling about Apaches, it didn't take much for me to figure out what you was telling him. Now, I don't know how many of 'em you got coming, but they won't get here in time to do you no good, any more'n Pino would if he was by hisself."

"Apaches can ride faster than you think," she said confidently. "And they can follow any trail, no matter how you might try to hide it."

Foxx saw Lita's scheme at once. Every minute that she could delay him with idle discussion was a minute gained for Pino and his allies. He said curtly, "I ain't going to waste time palavering with you, Lita. Come on. Let's get started."

"Where are we going, Foxx?" she asked, her eyes wide and innocent.

"You'll find out when we get there." Foxx took her arm and started to lead her to her horse.

"Wait, Foxx," she said. "I hurt my foot while I was struggling with you. I cannot walk quickly."

"Then I'll carry you," Foxx snapped. He moved to pick her up, but Lita still held back. He said, "Now, you better make up your mind how you're going to play your hand, Lita. You can try to slow us down, and that'll make me have to handle you pretty rough. Or you can behave yourself and make things easy for both of us."

Lita did not move or speak but stood staring at him. When Foxx saw that she was not going to reply, he took her wrist, and she let herself fall limply to the ground. Foxx still held her arm. He dragged her the few feet to the horse and let her lie at his feet while he took out his knife and sawed through three of the long rawhide strings that dangled from the saddle.

Lita did not speak but glowered at Foxx angrily while he bound her wrists in front of her. She let him lift her into her saddle and watched with curiosity while he looped a rawhide strip around each of her booted ankles and tied them to the shanks of her stirrups.

Stepping back, Foxx lighted a stogie while he studied Lita's bonds. He nodded and told her, "I don't think you'll be too bad off. We'll ride on, soon as I get mounted."

Leading Lita's horse, Foxx went back to where his own mount stood. He lifted the horse's foot and after a few strong twists pumped with adrenaline got the already loosened nail out of the animal's hoof. Tying the reins of Lita's horse to one of his saddle strings, Foxx mounted and started north, still following the trail left by Pepper and the gang led by Alvarez.

They rode in silence, Foxx glancing back now and then to make sure that Lita was not trying to break free. She ignored him each time he looked, staring ahead with her lips pressed into a straight, angry line and her eyes slitted against the glare of sunlight from the tan earth, the heat increasing now as the sun mounted steadily higher.

They'd been on the trail less than an hour when Foxx began to get distress signals from his stomach. With a start he realized that the morning was gone and he had not eaten since noon the preceding day. He'd intended to push on until he caught up with Pepper or Alvarez's gang or both, but he knew now that they must stop. Foxx headed for a rock overhang at the edge of a low mesa a quarter of a mile ahead, which offered a thin line of shade.

"We'll stop here to eat a bite," he told Lita when they reached the overhang. "I don't expect you took time for breakfast before you and Pino had taken out after me this morning."

"I am not hungry," she snapped.

"Suit yourself. If you ain't going to eat, there's no use in me letting you get off your horse, then."

Foxx took smoked sausage and cheese and crackers out of his saddlebag, lifted his canteen from the saddlehorn, and sat down in the thin patch of shade cast by the overhang. He unwrapped the food and cut pieces of sausage and cheese and started to eat. He did not look directly at Lita but managed to get a glimpse of her now and then as he casually watched the landscape. A thin line of perspiration beaded her upper lip, and he knew she must be very uncomfortable sitting in the hot sun. He tilted the canteen to take a sip of water between bites of sausage and looked up in time to see her turning her eyes away from him.

She did not break her silence at first. Not until

Foxx had finished his first thick slice of sausage and eaten most of a slab of cheese did she look directly at him. Foxx caught her gaze when he looked up. He smiled.

"Too bad you ain't hungry," he said before taking a bite from a second slice of sausage. "It's going to be a long time before we stop again."

Lita waited several minutes longer before she said, "Foxx, I have changed my mind. I would like something to eat."

It had not been Foxx's idea to punish Lita but only to drive home to her that she was dependent on him for food and water. He let the idea sink in while he finished chewing, then got up and untied her feet. She did not object when he held her arm while she dismounted, and held her elbow to steady her while she walked to the shade.

"You'll have to eat with your hands tied," he said, handing her sausage and cheese and crackers. "And eat fast, now. I don't aim to wait for you when I'm ready to ride again."

Lita looked at Foxx narrowly as she took the food he handed her. She said, "You are a smarter one than I took you to be, Foxx. It is a mistake I made, underestimating you."

"I didn't give you real high marks either," Foxx told her with a grim little smile. "Of course, I didn't know then that you was Pino's sister."

Lita had been eating eagerly while Foxx talked. She waited to swallow before saying, "Pino is too young to remember all the wisdom of our father But in the day when Mangas Coloradas was a name that brought fear to all, I listened many times while my father instructed his warriors how a battle was to be fought, or a raid carried out. And my memory is very good."

"Don't it ever get under your skin when you got to stand by and watch Pino and his crew mess things up?"

"They make mistakes only when they don't follow my orders, or when I am not on hand to tell them what to do," Lita snapped angrily. "If things were only different—" She sighed and shrugged her shoulders. "But they are not."

"After I seen your brother and Otero and Alvarez in action, I got the idea there was somebody with more sense than any of 'em behind all of this," Foxx said thoughtfully. "I wouldn't've picked you out being the one, though, Lita. But I reckon it ain't easy for a woman to get out in front and lead a rough bunch like a man can do."

"Don't talk like a fool, Foxx!" she snapped, her voice harsh with anger. "I could not control the Apaches. Their tradition forbids a woman to fight at the side of the men, and they would never agree to obey a woman who tried to lead them."

"You keep talking about the Apaches." Foxx frowned. "I got a hunch you're spinning me a yarn about 'em. You sure that ain't what you're doing, Lita? Because aside from them six or seven at the castle, I sure ain't seen none of 'em."

"That is only because their main force is not here yet. Oh, I do not have to lie to you, Foxx! Victorio is on his way, and he is bringing his brave warriors with him! When they have done their work, all of Arizona

Territory south of the Gila will once more belong to the Apacheria, and that is only a start! When we are through, all you whites will be dead as far north as this place where we are sitting now!"

CHAPTER 13

Foxx stared at Lita incredulously. He said, "You don't expect me to believe that, Lita! Why, Mangas Coloradas never did make a real big dent in the Territory. Neither did Cochise, when you come right down to it. This Victorio fellow you said something about just now, I ain't heard much about him yet."

"You will hear more," Lita said confidently. "Pino and I will help him by telling him the things we learned from Mangas, and he will unite all the Apacheria behind him."

"Well, no Indians ever did hang together long enough to do much before," Foxx said, recalling the tribal ill feelings of his Comanche days, when Kotsoteka sneered at Yamparika, Yamparika at Kwahadi, and Kwahadi at Penetaka. "You ain't never going to get the Chiricahuas and the Mescaleros and the Coyoteros and all them other little bunches to set down and eat out of the same pot, let alone fight together."

"Victorio will unite them!" Lita insisted.

Ignoring her interruption, Foxx went on, "Besides, there's a lot more soldiers out here now than there ever was in Mangas Coloradas's day."

"We Apaches spit on your army, Foxx! This is our land, and in it your soldiers are as children!"

"It ain't going to be that way very much longer. Soldiers might talk a little bit longer to learn a lesson than some folks, but once they learn it, they don't forget. And when the railroads get through building, it's going to be a lot easier for the soldiers to move around, remember."

"Your railroads do not frighten us either!" Lita said contemptuously. "We take money from one to fight another, and when only one is left, we will fight it!"

"Wait a minute!" Foxx broke in. "Are you telling me that another railroad's paying your outfit to raid the C&K?"

"I only meant that our people make money working for your railroads, Foxx," Lita answered quickly. The wave of anger that had led her to speak so freely was passing now.

Foxx nodded as though her reply satisfied him, but he made a mental note of the indiscreet remark for later investigation. He said, "If you're done eating, we'll move on."

"Where are you taking me, Foxx? To the construction camp?"

Foxx shook his head. "You'll find out when we get to where we're going. But I've got to see what happened to Pepper, so we'll keep on following Alvarez's tracks for right now."

"If you are wise, you will not waste time looking for your small friend," Lita said. "By this time Alvarez will have caught up with him and be on his way back to the hacienda with a new scalp to put into our chest."

"Pepper's able to look out for hisself," Foxx said curtly. He got to his feet and started gathering up the food that was left from their meal.

"Even if he escapes Alvarez now, Victorio will get him. Just as he will get you, too." Lita looked at Foxx and with her bound hands made a clumsy gesture of scalping. "Oh, yes! Your scalp will be ours, too, and soon!"

Foxx stared at her for a moment before asking the question that had been on his mind since he'd learned her true identity. He asked her, "You mind telling me something?"

Lita shrugged. "I have told you so much when anger loosened my tongue that a bit more foolishness will make no difference. What is it you want to know?"

"Feeling like you do about white men, why'd you come to my room the other night, Lita?"

Lita smiled. "It will do no harm to tell you the truth. I came to you for two reasons, Foxx. One was that I needed a man that night."

"With all them men back there at your big house? I ain't about to believe that, Lita!"

"It is true," she insisted. "I do not bed with them! If I did, they would begin to look on me as their property, and then I would not be able to command them, even speaking through Pino!"

Foxx nodded thoughtfully. "Well, I guess that makes sense."

"On things of no importance I do not trouble myself to lie," Lita said arrogantly. "When I came to you, I had been too long without a man, and you were the one I saw who attracted me the most." She hesitated, then added, "And I have said I will be truthful, so I will tell you that I did enjoy you. You know how to please a woman, Foxx."

Foxx waited until he could see that she was not going to continue before he asked, "You said there was two reasons. Are you going to tell me the other one?"

"From what Alvarez told me after you killed his companion in La Paz, I knew you were going to be our chief enemy. Can you tell me of a better way to find out what your enemy is like than to go to bed with him?"

"Well, if you was looking for a way to show me where I stand, you sure found it," Foxx told her. He did not speak angrily for Lita's candor had taken much of the sting out of her words. "I'll give you credit for not being mealymouthed about it, though. Now, let's get moving again. We wasted too much time already."

Foxx led Lita's horse, as before, when they moved out, heading north again on the trail left by Alvarez's men and by Pepper before them. The tracks grew erratic now. Before Pepper had traveled in an almost straight line; he was veering now, first to the northeast, then to the northwest. Each time Pepper had changed his course, Alvarez's men had changed theirs. Foxx stopped more than once to study the ground, trying to puzzle out Pepper's motive in taking such a zigzag course, but no reason that he could think of made sense to him.

They stopped at a dry wash to rest the horses and to drink from Foxx's canteen. Foxx dismounted, but left Lita on her horse; he led the two horses behind him while he walked along the shallow gully studying the maze of hoofprints and boot prints that broke the earth along its bottom and sides.

Here Pepper's tracks were not as overlaid as elsewhere by those of Alvarez's gang. They showed that the little man had left his horse to scout up and down the gully on foot, then had cut back on his own trail, in an apparent effort to confuse his pursuers by circling behind them.

In his haste to catch up to Pepper, Alvarez seemed to have fallen for the ruse. From the aimless pattern of hoofprints in the wash and leading to it and away from it, Foxx read the confusion that had followed when Alvarez lost Pepper's trail. He had split his force into three groups, sending one pair east, anther west, and the third straight ahead, in an effort to find their quarry's trail again. Foxx stopped and lighted a stogie while he made up his mind which set of Apache tracks to follow.

"It will end soon," Lita said as she watched Foxx examining the ground. "Your small friend is running now like the deer when the hunters make a circle and close in on it. But the deer can find no opening in the circle through which it can break. In a little while we will find his body."

"He's kept away from your bunch so far," Foxx replied with a new confidence in his voice. Lita's interpretation of what the tracks showed did not agree with the conclusion Foxx had reached. He added, "I don't imagine he'll have much trouble slipping away from 'em awhile longer."

Pepper had held his own quite well, and because the tracks had been shifting consistently but almost imperceptibly to the east, Foxx had an idea what had been going through Pepper's mind. He mounted and started moving northeast. For the first time since leaving the castle, he did not follow any of the hoofprints that pocked the soil all around the dry wash.

All the backtracking and changing of directions they'd done since stopping to eat had taken up a good part of the afternoon. They had ridden for perhaps an hour since leaving the dry wash and were well into the Hualapai foothills, and the land was becoming rougher and more broken when Foxx got his first intimation of danger.

Distantly to the west he saw two horsemen, riding at an angle that would intercept him and Lita if he kept moving straight ahead. The tracks at the dry wash had shown that Alvarez had divided his men into two groups of two and one group of three. Foxx knew that the two approaching on the western horizon were almost certainly one of the renegade pairs.

Lita had seen the horsemen at the same time that Foxx did. She said, "It will not be long before I am free now, Foxx. If they are so close, the others cannot be far away."

Although Foxx had already reached the same conclusion, he ignored Lita's comment. He increased the pace of the horses to a faster walk and changed their course to stay parallel with the distant riders.

Foxx could tell at once when the pair spotted

them. The men speeded up and swung around to intercept them. He responded by urging his own and Lita's horse to a faster pace.

Lita had seen the riders change course, too. A note of gloating in her voice, she said, "Grass and Stenache have seen us now. They will not let you get away from them, Foxx. You waste time trying."

"Grass and Stenache, they're them two riding for us now?"

"Yes. They are two to your one. As soon as they catch up to us, it will all be over."

"Like you said, it's only two against one," Foxx replied calmly. "I'll take my chances."

Notwithstanding his calm reply, Foxx knew that time was short. He'd been scanning the terrain ahead, looking for a place which would offer them cover and at the same time give him a position to defend. He needed to find a low hump or blind draw, where one man could stand off seven.

There were few such places in the broken land that lay directly ahead of them, but a half-mile to the east Foxx saw a tiny isolated mesa. It was too small really to be dignified by the name, but that in itself could be an advantage, he knew. The squat column of earth and rock stood up from a stretch of flatland like a big mushroom without the cap. With the terrain clear on all sides of it, one man might have a chance to hold his own, Foxx saw. He increased their pace and headed for the tiny plateau.

They reached it far ahead of the riders to the west of them. Foxx reined in and stood up in his stirrups to spot the riders who were still a comfortable distance away but had increased their pace and were closing in.

Foxx circled the mesa, looking for the easiest path to the top. There were only two passable ridges. Foxx chose the one which shouldered up abruptly like a ramp, providing a small triangular pocket between the ridge and the mesa's wall where the horses could be tethered. Lita had said nothing since their last bit of verbal sparring, but she had kept her eyes on Grass and Stenache while Foxx was leading her horse around the mesa's base.

Now she said, "Why should you die, Foxx? There is still time for you to join with us! I have been watching you—you'd make a good Apache, you know."

"I guess you're paying me a compliment," Foxx said dryly. "Even if it ain't one I care about. But I don't reckon I need to tell you what I think about your proposition."

"No. I knew you would refuse. But there is one thing you may not have thought of."

Foxx smiled a bit grimly. "I guess there's more'n one thing I ain't thought about, or I wouldn't be here. Go on, Lita. You feel like telling me what I overlooked?"

"Remember, I will need a man to stand beside me. You could be that man, Foxx! Think of it, while there is still time!"

"I don't need to think about it, Lita. I'd sooner bed down with a rattlesnake, if you want the truth. Now just keep quiet. I got too many things to do to jaw with you."

Foxx's rejection of her as a woman angered Lita

more than his earlier refusal. Her dark eyes snapped, her lips turned down, and she retorted, "You are a fool! When Grass and Stenache get here, they will shoot, and so will you. The others must be close enough now to hear the shooting, so they will come to see what is going on, and then it will be over very quickly."

Foxx did not bother to reply. He guided his horse into the little sheltered space, dismounted, and led Lita's horse up beside his. He tethered both horses to the biggest boulder he could find in the triangle, and left her sitting in her saddle while he carried his rifle, canteen, and saddlebags to the top of the mesa. He looked at the riders; they were little more than two miles distant by now and had not slackened their pace.

He watched them for a moment, gauging the time he had left, then turned to go back to the horses for Lita. By instinct he swept his eyes around the horizon before starting down. To the southeast Foxx saw three more horsemen, and as closely as he could tell they, too, were heading for the mesa.

"You're going up on this hump, now," Foxx told Lita when he returned to the horses. "Promise me you'll behave, and I'll let you walk up there like a lady. If you don't, I'll toss you over my shoulder and tote you like a sack of potatoes. Now, which way are you going to pick out?"

"I'll walk," she replied. "But don't expect me to go any further in helping you, Foxx."

"I don't. Whatever's done, I can take care of it without looking for you to help me."

Back atop the mesa, Foxx checked the progress of

Stenache and Grass; they were a quarter of a hour's ride distant now. He looked for a safe place to leave Lita. The spot Foxx had chosen to defend was small, a roughly circular area not more than thirty feet across at its widest part. The top was bare and relatively level, though it came to a blunt tip close to its center. A few shallow erosion creases ran from the center to the edges, and he picked the deepest of these as a place for Lita to stay.

"If you lay down in this run and keep low, it ain't likely you'll be hit," he told her, indicating the trough.

"I was mistaken about you, Foxx," Lita said. Her lips were turned up in a mocking smile, but her voice was serious. "You would never make an Apache."

"Not that I'd want to, but how do you figure I wouldn't?"

"An Apache wouldn't be worrying about me being safe. He'd be planning to use me as a shield when the bullets start flying."

"Maybe you ought not to've told me that. I just might decide to do it."

Lita smiled thinly as she shook her head. "No. I know there's no danger you'd ever do that, Foxx. If I'd thought there was, I'd have kept quiet."

"Don't make no mistake about one thing," he warned. "Woman or not, if you get in my way or try to run, it won't hurt me one bit to put a bullet into you."

"I believe that." She nodded.

"You'll keep still then?"

"I've made all the promises I'm going to make, Foxx. I promise you nothing more."

Foxx stared narrowly at Lita for a moment, wondering why she had chosen to give him the answer she did when it would have been so easy to lie instead. Finally he said, "If you feel that way, it's all right with me. You know I'll be keeping an eye on you all the time. Now, lay down and stay still. I got a few more little jobs to do."

There were no real positions for Foxx to defend on the mesa; he had seen that at his first glance around its summit. It did not offer a bulwark that would shield him from bullets fired by one of the attackers. The only real advantage of the mesa was that at no point within rifle range was it overlooked by higher ground.

Foxx stood for a moment in the center of the mesa, taking mental notes of the present positions of his assailants. Grass and Stenache would be within rifle range within the next few minutes. Shortly after the first shots were fired, the other three would arrive.

He spent the little time remaining before Grass and Stenache got close in moving around the mesa's perimeter, depositing small handfuls of the supply of rifle ammunition he carried in his saddlebags at a half-dozen points. Foxx did not want to haul his saddlebags with him as he moved around the top of the mesa, nor could he afford to risk being caught anywhere with the Winchester's magazine empty.

After he'd completed the circuit, Foxx sat down facing the west and waited for Stenache and Grass to come within range. They were still too far away for him to see their features, but they were close enough for him to see one of them pointing out his position to the other. Foxx took out a twisted stogie, put a match to it, and puffed calmly, watching the smoke rise straight up into the windless sky while he waited for the approaching riders to come within range.

Grass and Stenache were not fools, but Foxx had not expected them to be. They pulled up outside of rifle range and sat for a moment, pointing and nodding, as they made their plan. It was about what Foxx had anticipated. Grass wheeled his horse and rode north, obviously heading for the other side of the mesa so as to force Foxx to split his attention between them. Stenache stayed in place, his head uptilted as he watched.

Foxx did not move. He sat and waited, calmly puffing the stogie. The little cigar had been reduced to a stub before a shot sounded behind him. Foxx had anticipated the shot, too. He gave Stenache the satisfaction of seeing him move to the west side of the mesa, where he watched Grass long enough to estimate the time he would take to ride within range. Then Foxx dropped to his belly on the hard ground and got Stenache in the Winchester's sights.

Apaches did not fight comfortably from horseback, as the Comanches did. They followed the style of mounted infantry, who used horses to take them to the battle scene, then dismounted and did their fighting on foot.

Stenache had learned one Comanche trick, though. As he came within rifle range of the mesa, he turned his horse until he was riding at an angle to its side and dropped behind the animal. Now he was shielded by the horse's body, and Foxx's target was reduced to Stenache's arm, around the horse's neck, or the leg which the Apache had draped across his saddle.

There was only one flaw in Stenache's tactic. In his position behind his horse, clinging to the animal's mane with one hand, Stenache had no way at all to get off an aimed bullet at Foxx as long as the horse was moving.

Foxx was quick to take advantage of the opportunity. He belly-crawled to the east side of the mesa until he could see Grass. The renegade was coming at a gallop, riding upright, his rifle in one hand, reins in the other, his horse's mane and tail streaming in the wake of its self-created breeze.

Foxx was in no hurry to shoot and had no ammunition to waste. He followed his target with the Winchester's muzzle, keeping Grass's broad chest in its sights, until he was sure of the lead he'd need for a telling shot. In as leisurely a fashion as though he was target shooting, Foxx squeezed off the round. The bullet took Grass squarely. He reared back in the saddle, held his position for a few seconds, then toppled to the ground.

Foxx felt neither guilt nor pleasure. He knew he had made a good shot and had halved the number of his enemies. He glanced at Grass's riderless mustang, still galloping toward the mesa, and quickly revised upward the number of his assailants. Coming at full tilt and now almost within rifle range were the three renegades who such a short time ago had seemed so safely distant.

There was no time to waste, and Foxx wasted none. He snaked back to the opposite side of the mesa. Stenache was not in the place where Foxx had expected him to be. The Apache had reversed his position on the horse and turned the animal, and he was now riding toward the mesa at an angle that would within a few moments take him out of Foxx's sight under the edge of the mesa's rim.

Foxx started wriggling toward the rim but saw the barrel of Stenache's rifle sticking up above the horse's body and knew that the Indian was waiting for him to show himself. At such close range Foxx assumed Stenache could handle a rifle like a handgun, even from the cramped position in which the Apache was holding himself.

Stenache drew himself up over the horse's back, and aimed and fired in the split second he saw Foxx's head in his rifle sights. Foxx rolled back as he saw Stenache pulling himself up. His move was not a second too soon. Stenache's slug whistled through the air past Foxx's ear.

Foxx had no time to fire before the Apache was out of sight under the mesa's rim; out of range unless Foxx hung over the rim and made himself an easy target. The defense line that Foxx had thought safe had been breached. He now had an enemy who could reach him simply by walking up the ridge to the top of the mesa.

Foxx was still lying on his belly, staring at the rim, when the soft grating of feet behind him brought his head around. Lita stood over him, a long knife raised in her hand.

CHAPTER 14

Lita started to bring the knife down. Foxx rolled aside, catching her ankles with his legs and tripping her. She toppled, but extended an arm to break her fall and landed on her knees. When Foxx lifted himself into a sitting position, he saw her kneeling in front of him, holding the weapon low in the style of a skilled knife-fighter, the blade edge-up, ready for an upward stab or a sidewise slash. Foxx brought up his knees to protect himself when Lita swept the blade in a bold arc, her target his abdomen. The knife glanced off the tough hide of his water-buffalo boots, and Lita's hand was deflected downward.

Foxx tried to stamp on her hand as it touched the ground, but Lita pulled it back before his boot sole touched her. She lurched forward, thrusting like a fencer, the point of the blade going for Foxx's crotch. Foxx raised his foot. Lita collided with it, and the impact stopped her at the midpoint of her lunge, her breast pressed to Foxx's boot sole. He kicked mercilessly, and she fell backward, still holding the knife. His kick must have hurt her, but the cry that burst from her throat was not one of pain; it sounded like the snarl of an enraged panther.

A shot rang out from the ground, and lead whistled over the top of the mesa. Foxx did not notice the direction from which the shot had been fired. His attention was fixed on the wild-eyed woman who had sprung up to face him. He sat on the ground watching for a moment when he could get to his feet without giving her a chance to reach him with her blade.

Lita paid no more attention to the shot than Foxx had. She took a small step forward, and Foxx shifted his balance in anticipation of another lunge. Lita saw that he was ready for her attack and stopped short. The print of Foxx's boot sole showed as a dark spot on the tan fabric of her charro jacket; it covered one breast, and Foxx knew that he must have hurt her.

Hurt or not, Lita was ready to press her attack. She leaped around to come at Foxx from the side, but he rolled away from her as she jumped, and this time was able to complete the roll in a quick spring that brought him to his feet. They faced each other across a yard of space, and Lita took a step, bending from the waist as she moved, the knife point coming up from the level of Foxx's thighs.

Quick as Lita's thrust was, Foxx's hand was quicker. It darted forward like a striking rattlesnake, and his strong fingers clamped tightly on Lita's wrist. He did not try to push her back but shoved down on her arm as she lunged and at the same time pulled her toward him and twirled her around so that her back was toward him. As he pulled Lita's wrist up into the small of her back, Foxx's thumb found the vulnerable nerve in her wrist. He dug his thumb into the tender spot until the knife dropped from her numbed fingers.

Foxx picked up the wicked shining blade without easing the pressure of his hold on Lita's wrist. He was angry, more at himself than at her, for he knew how lax he had been in failing to search Lita. He felt stupid for having overlooked her boot top, as often as he'd used his own boot as a hiding place for his Cloverleaf Colt. Then a rifle spoke from the ground, and he dropped flat, pulling Lita with him.

Foxx maintained his grip as they fell, and sprawled on top of Lita's body, anchoring her facedown to the ground. Lita did not struggle, and Foxx used the lull to look about him, seeking the source of the shots.

He saw that the three riders coming from the southeast were now within rifle range. They were lined up, gazing at the top of the mesa. Foxx saw one of them raise his rifle. He pulled his head down an instant before the report of the shot sounded and the bullet whistled over them.

Lita was still lying facedown, Foxx's body half-across her. She pushed her shoulder up and looked to see where the shot had come from, then twisted her head to look at Foxx. A grim smile was on her lips.

"It is Alvarez, with Chato and Eusebio," she told him. "Now you are beaten, Foxx! You cannot stop them by yourself!"

"No, but I can make a good try," he replied levelly. "Which is what I aim to do."

Their movements had brought Lita's head within view of the snipers from below, giving them a target, and they let off a ragged volley. One slug went high, singing angrily over the heads of Foxx and Lita; the other two bullets hit short and kicked up dust at the rim of the mesa.

Foxx pushed his shoulder down, pinning Lita to the ground again. He grated, "That was a fool trick! Them fellows down below are shooting at anything they see move up here! They can't tell whether it's you or me!"

"It was worth trying," Lita panted. "A bullet hole would be a small exchange for your life, Foxx!"

"Well, you didn't make it. And there's a lot of questions I want to ask you yet, so I got to keep you alive. Now, you bend over when we get up and run back to where I put you when we first come up here!"

"Carry me!" she spat back at him.

"Carry, hell!" he snorted in reply.

Foxx began crawfishing across the mesa's rough surface, crawling backward, dragging Lita toward the gully, but after they'd moved a few feet, she saw he would not stop or be more gentle with her. She used her hands and knees then to speed their forward progress.

They reached the little gully. Foxx looked at the severed remains of the leather strips he had bound her with. They were now useless. He was still holding the knife. He pulled up Lita's split riding skirt and cut the hems off both sides. Pressing a knee in the small of her back to hold her facedown, Foxx used the strips he'd cut to tie Lita's wrists behind her, then lashed her ankles together and rolled her over on her side into the gully.

There had been no shots from below for several moments, but Foxx had not forgotten that Stenache was footloose somewhere at the bottom of the mesa. He went to his belly again and crawled to where his rifle lay, picked it up, and started a crawling tour of the perimeter of the mesa, working himself as close to the edge as he dared. He looked first at the horses, saw they were safe, and crawled on.

As he moved slowly along the curving southern rim, a bullet threw up a spurt of dust just in front of him. Foxx rolled away from the rim, and as he moved got a fleeting glimpse of still another pair of horsemen. They'd pulled up just inside the rifle range, but their faces were little more than blurs. Foxx deduced they must be Guevavi and Augusto, since Grass, Stenache, Alvarez, Chato, and Eusebio were already accounted for.

"Well," Foxx muttered as he gazed at the newcomers, "all I need now is for Victorio's bunch of Apaches to show up."

He took another look around. The newest arrivals were moving now, but they were not riding toward him. They had withdrawn from their earlier position and were still safely out of rifle range. They rode in an arc that kept them parallel with the wall of the mesa, going to join Alvarez and his men, who themselves were also retreating from rifle range.

Foxx did not have to guess what was in the wind. It was all too obvious that they would make plans for surrounding the mesa and launching a concerted attack from several points. He looked at the sun and shook his head. It was low in the sky by now, but he estimated that he'd have more than an hour to wait until the sun dropped below the western horizon.

Taking advantage of the time that would pass before the gang had an organized plan to put into effect, Foxx completed his circuit of the mesa's rim. Twice he risked crawling to the very edge and peering straight down, but there was no sign of Stenache or his horse. The body of Grass still lay huddled where Foxx had brought him down; the dead renegade's horse stood near by.

Stenache on the prowl was not a prospect that Foxx liked to contemplate, but the worry that gnawed at his mind was soon relieved. When he'd finished his circle of the mesa, he took a final look to the southeast to see what progress was being made in the council of war. He saw four men instead of three waiting for the two who were still approaching them. Stenache, he concluded, must have been summoned by Alvarez to join the others.

"What has happened to Alvarez, Foxx?" Lita called from the gully. "You have not shot, and neither have his men. Surely they haven't gone?"

"Oh, they're still out there," Foxx assured her. "Just out of range. The shooting's over for a while."

"It will start again, very soon," she promised. "They will not give up until they have killed or captured you."

"I wouldn't count on it. Alvarez and his scalp-takers weren't smart enough to keep me from getting away from that castle of yours, and I'll handle 'em just as easy out here."

Lita did not answer for several moments. The

silence started her thinking. At last she said, "You have forgotten Victorio's Apaches. Pino should be on the way with them by now."

"I ain't forgot 'em. But I won't worry about no Apaches until I see 'em."

"Be a fool, then!" Lita exclaimed. "You will see them soon enough. Victorio sent a runner ahead of him. The runner came to the hacienda yesterday, with word that Victorio was only a day behind him. They will be here, do not think otherwise!"

Foxx glanced up at the sun and said, "If they don't get here in the next hour, there won't be time for 'em to do much before it's dark. And six men can't cover every inch of ground around this mesa, so maybe I'll have time to give that gang of yours the slip and get us out of here after all."

Lita spat. "Victorio's men are pure Apaches, Foxx! They have eyes like the cat and fight better in the dark than they do in daylight!"

"We'll just take our chances, then," Foxx told her. "If I was you, Lita, I'd sure be wishing them Apaches could see in the dark as good as you say they do."

Lita frowned, the meaning of his words escaping her. "Why?"

"Because you'll be going out with me when it's time. It'd be a downright shame if them Apaches of yours killed you in the dark by mistake."

Lita did not reply; she was looking at Alvarez and his group, who still sat their horses, close together, to the southeast of the mesa. Foxx busied himself lighting a stogie. He was flicking out the match when a muffled exclamation burst from Lita's throat.

"Ah, good! Look, Foxx! They are arriving, Victorio and his men! Look, there, beyond where Alvarez is!"

Foxx looked and saw riders coming in single file through the broken foothills to the southeast. The familiar figure of Pino, his gold-embroidered charro jacket gleaming in the yellow rays of the declining sun, threw off bright reflections.

Behind him came the Apaches, their brown torsos erect on their saddleless mounts. They wore only breechclouts and moccasins, their long hair was cut off straight just above their shoulders, and all of them wore headbands to keep their eyes free during the heat of battle. Lita reared up eagerly to see, her bound wrists forcing her to wriggle and raise her body like a seal on an ice floe.

Foxx and Lita watched in silence as a half-dozen Apaches came into view. Then the file ended; no more riders were in sight. Foxx asked, "Is that all the men Victorio's got?"

Lita's voice was a hoarse whisper loaded with worry as she replied, "Of course not! He has more than a hundred warriors under his command. They will follow soon, you will see!"

They waited, watching in silence, while Pino and the Apache band drew closer. Pino was close to Alvarez and his group now, but still no more Apaches came into view.

Skepticism in his voice, Foxx told Lita, "Looks like you're in for a big letdown. If there was any more Apaches besides them that we can already see, they'd've been in sight by now."

"Something has delayed them," Lita replied. "Victorio must have brought more than that small handful!"

"You know Victorio, I guess," Foxx said. "You see him in that bunch coming up?"

Lita had not taken her eyes off the short file of Indian horsemen. She shook her head. Her voice a hoarse whisper, she answered, "No. He must be coming with the main band."

"It don't look to me like there's going to be any main band, Lita," Foxx said levelly. "I got a hunch you're looking at all the Apaches he figured you was worth."

"That is not so!" Lita insisted.

"If any more was coming, they'd sure be in sight by now."

Lita had kept her eyes fixed on the horizon, and when the landscape remained empty, she shrugged and slumped down once more to lie in the gully.

Her voice carefully casual, she reminded Foxx, "Even if no more arrive, there are enough now to join Alvarez in taking this mesa and setting me free!"

During his verbal sparring with Lita, Foxx had been watching the merging of the Apaches with Alvarez's men while Lita had devoted her attention to the horizon. Alvarez's men and the Apaches had wasted little time in discussion; there had been only a brief period of talk accompanied by pointing and gesturing as the men from the castle explained the lay of the land to the Indians. Now they milled around as they turned their horses. In a single long line the twelve riders started at a gallop for the mesa.

"I guess we're about to find out," Foxx told Lita calmly. "It'll be right interesting to find out if them

Apaches you been bragging about are as good as you make 'em out to be."

"I pity you, Foxx!" she retorted, but there was no trace of pity or sympathy in her voice. "What you find out will be the last lesson you will learn!"

Foxx turned away without answering. He walked to the southeast rim of the mesa and watched while the gap between the line of horsemen and the mesa began closing. The attackers were still out of range of Foxx's Winchester, but he knew that his best and perhaps only chance of surviving an attack against odds of a dozen to one was to get in the first shots and to make each of those early bullets count.

Stretching out prone beside the little pile of ammunition he'd put in place earlier, Foxx cradled his Winchester to his shoulder and waited.

He sighted on the man in the center of the line as the riders galloped toward him. His finger was on the trigger and he was beginning the deliberate squeeze that would send his first bullet when the riders parted.

Without breaking stride the four men on the left end of the advancing cavalcade wheeled to the north. At the same time the remaining eight turned south. Foxx swung his rifle, trying to keep it on the target he'd selected, but the sudden change threw his aim off. He missed.

He brought the rifle around and found the end rider in his sights, and this time his shot went home. The Apache tumbled off his galloping horse and lay still.

Foxx saw at once what his enemies had planned. By splitting their force, putting a majority of their firepower on the south, they intended to pin Foxx down by keeping him busy holding off the larger group, which would allow the four men on the opposite side to dash in quickly and storm the mesa. They knew as well as Foxx did that he would be forced to spend most of his time on the force that had the greatest threat. Though the top of the mesa was small, Foxx could not dash from one side to the other quickly enough or maintain a volume of shots heavy enough on one side or the other to be a real threat to either group.

"It's damned if you do, damned if you don't," Foxx muttered to himself, his head swiveling as he looked from one party of attackers to the other. "There ain't much real choice, but I got to take care of the big bunch first."

He was already belly-crawling to the south side of the mesa as he spoke. He reached it in time to see the larger of the two attacking forces pulling away to extreme rifle range. He sent a token shot or two after the riders, missing both times, before it came home to him that since they'd made their latest move, his enemies had not fired a single shot. Angry with himself for not having seen the attackers' secondary strategy before, Foxx put his rifle aside to diminish the temptation to fire uselessly.

Now the tempting began. The large force facing Foxx had formed a rough semicircle at extreme rifle range from the mesa. From each end of the straggling line, riders came out. Both were Apaches. They galloped in zigzags toward Foxx's position, waving their rifles over their heads.

Instinctively Foxx reached for his rifle but quickly

drew back his hand. He set himself to wait and see which of the two men was the real attacker and which was the decoy before he shot. He knew that one of them would get temptingly close to the mesa to draw his fire, and while Foxx concentrated on the decoy, the second would try for an effective shot.

When Foxx failed to take their bait, the two riders circled for a moment, keeping in constant motion to lessen their chances of taking a bullet if Foxx did decide to fire. Then they resumed their zigzag advance. Foxx waited until he was reasonably sure of a hit. He followed the erratic antics of the Apache on his left until he did not dare wait any longer for fear the man would realize how close he'd come to the mesa and turn back. Then he squeezed off a shot. The slug went home, and the Apache fell.

As though Foxx's shot or the Apache's dropping from his horse were a signal, the other riders began firing. Bullets buzzed with angry whines above Foxx's prone figure, and a few plowed into the dirt on either side of him. Foxx pressed himself as flat as possible and waited for the volume of shooting to diminish.

It was a relatively short volley, and it soon faded to an occasional desultory shot. Foxx risked raising his head high enough to look across the stretch of raw earth between the base of the mesa and the horsemen. The attacking force was withdrawing, but the Apache who'd advanced from the right-hand end of the line was galloping before the south base of the mesa to pick up the man Foxx had shot.

For a moment the attackers held their fire. The Apache Foxx had shot had not moved after hitting the ground, but as the second Indian reached him and leaned over with his arm stretched to the ground, the wounded man grasped the outstretched hand and swung up on the horse's cruppers. Both men sat erect as the horse galloped on without breaking stride. Foxx waited, seeing the man he thought he had just killed ride out of range of his rifle.

A scraping of earth behind Foxx broke the silence. He raised his head to look back, and saw a breach-clout-clad Apache running for the north rim of the mesa—with Lita across one shoulder. Lying as he was on his stomach, Foxx could not draw his revolver. He reached for his rifle, but before he could bring it around, the man had leaped down to the ridge which Foxx had used as a ramp and was gone.

Ignoring the occasional shot that was still coming from the men lined up south of the mesa, Foxx crouched and ran across to check on the horses. He drew his S&W as he ran, but when he looked down, the Indian carrying Lita had disappeared. Both horses were gone from the improvised corral.

Foxx heard the quick drumming of hoofbeats, but the horses and riders were out of sight around the curve of the mesa's base. He hurried to the edge. The Apache who had rescued Lita had thrown her across the back of her horse and was leading it at a gallop toward the east. Riding as a screen between him and the mesa were the three men who'd made up the party. One of them was leading Foxx's horse.

Foxx brought up his revolver and let off two quick shots. The first one missed, but the second took one of the riders in the back. From his clothing Foxx identified him as one of the Apaches belonging to Alvarez's gang, but he could not see the man's face.

One of Victorio's Apaches pulled up abreast of the wounded man, leaned over and grabbed the horse's reins, and rode on, the two horses pressed close, the Apache steadying the wounded man. The maneuver had not slowed the party's retreat. Foxx fired again, but the group was beyond the accurate range of his Smith & Wesson by the time he'd gotten the shot off.

Shooting from the attacking party to the south of the mesa had stopped now. Foxx risked standing up to look in that direction and saw that the group was riding to the northeast, on an interception course with the smaller group that had carried out Lita's rescue.

It was evident to Foxx that the two groups had made no plans beyond getting Lita out of his hands. Now they were assembling to launch a final assault on the mesa. Given the odds which he now faced, even with the man he'd killed and the pair he'd wounded, Foxx knew the attack on his improvised fortress could hardly fail to succeed and that he could expect no mercy from the men who would carry it out.

Going to his saddlebags, Foxx took out the bottle of Cyrus Noble, wrapped in his spare shirt to protect it while he was traveling. He unswathed the bottle and took a long, thoughtful swallow. Slowly, almost absentmindedly, he took a cigar from his pocket and lighted it.

Looking at the mixture of Apaches and renegades that had gathered east of the mesa, Foxx noticed his shadow. It stretched almost to the rim of the little mesa, and the shadow of the mesa itself on the broken ground beyond it had become visible for the first time.

"If I can hold 'em off just a little while," he muttered, "I might have a chance to pull a sneak when it gets good and dark."

Methodically Foxx set about making his preparations. The job was a simple one and took only a few minutes to complete. He had a clue to the way his assailants were likely to think from the plan they'd used in the rescue attempt. He picked up the rifle ammunition he'd deposited around the rim of the mesa and divided it into two piles. He put one of the piles on the north rim, the other on the south. From his saddlebags he took the box of spare cartridges for the Smith & Wesson and the Colt Cloverleaf and emptied them into his pockets, .38's in his right-hand pocket, .41's for the Cloverleaf in his left. That done, Foxx sat down in the center of the mesa with a stogie in his mouth and the bottle of Noble in one hand and waited.

CHAPTER 15

Foxx waited, impatient to be back in action yet hoping his enemies would delay their attack until darkness was near enough to give him at least a gambler's chance of getting away.

He watched the council of war that the renegades and Apaches were holding and wondered why it was being dragged out such a long time. Then he remembered how the Comanche councils went on and on, and it occurred to him that Apache councils must be very similar, with each one present explaining at length why he opposed or supported the matter under debate. Usually each speaker had a different solution to propose, so a council might go on for several days.

This one lasted until only a narrow strip of bright yellow sky separated the sun from the western horizon. When it did end, the change from talk to action took place instantly. The cluster of renegades and

Apaches broke up into a loose group of horsemen, who started toward the mesa at a fast trot. Foxx looked for the glistening gold-trimmed jackets worn by Lita and Pino and soon spotted them, close together in the center of the group.

As they advanced, the riders spaced themselves out into a single line. The line quickly curved into a half-circle. Foxx saw that this time his assailants intended to form a ring completely encircling the mesa, so that he could not possibly cover all the points.

He looked again for the gold-trimmed jackets as the group moved into its new formation, and saw that Pino had gone to one end of the arc while Lita stayed near its center. As soon as the riders came within extreme rifle range, they kicked their mounts into a gallop and began shooting.

They did not fire as a military unit, in massed volleys, but in well-aimed single shots. Foxx dropped flat on the mesa's surface when the first bullet zipped past him, only inches away. He did not reply to the rifle shots. The range was too great for accuracy, and he knew that the only reason for these early shots was to draw him into returning his attackers' fire and using up ammunition that he would need badly later in the fight.

Foxx lay quietly, waiting for the horsemen to close the distance between their line and the mesa. He intended to make every one of his shots count. He was looking along the arch of the advancing line to choose his first target when he saw a strange vehicle lurch over a ridge a quarter-mile behind the attackers. It came down the low slope a few yards and stopped, then began moving again, heading for the mesa. The riders did not see it; their attention was concentrated on Foxx, and the shooting covered any noise the odd vehicle might be making.

Foxx thought of the odd thing as a wagon only because it rolled forward on wheels and was pulled by a four-horse team, though the monstrous contrivance had no visible driver. Its sides rose straight above the wheels four or five feet, and as far as Foxx could see, the wall surfaces were unbroken. It was simply a blocky rectangle on wheels without any marks to indicate where it came from or where it was headed.

Staring at the absurd-looking object which was drawing closer to the attackers' rear with every rotation of its four high wheels, Foxx held his fire. He was not sure just what he was looking at, but whatever it was, he saw that it might create a diversion that he could use to his advantage.

A bullet thudding into the ground only inches from Foxx's side reminded him that he was still under fire and that his assailants were getting close enough for accurate shooting. He sighted in on Lita, but her horse veered sharply and reared up on its hind legs just as he was squeezing off his shot. The horse fell, kicking spasmodically. Lita was thrown. She lay sprawled and motionless on the ground beside the horse.

Foxx shifted his attention to Pino. His cheek cuddled on the Winchester's smooth stock, he followed the flash of gold. He had his finger curled on the trigger and his sights fixed when one of the riders saw the wagon and let out a yell that could be heard over the spattering of shots. The attacking line broke as Apache and renegade alike turned to look, then reined in, wheeled their mounts, and spurred toward the slowly moving wagon.

It did not stop, and nothing happened until the first of the riders was within a dozen yards of the strange vehicle. Then a half-dozen flashes of muzzle blast spurted from the wagon's walls as the sharp crack of rifles and the flat, lower-toned spat of shotguns filled the air.

Panic gripped the attackers, although the shots caused more surprise than actual damage. The riders in front shielded the men and horses behind them, and only one of the attackers toppled from his horse, but the shotgun pellets sprayed the loosely spaced force and half the horses began to dance out of control. In an instant the area around the wagon became the scene of pandemonium.

When he saw the muzzle flashes and heard the shots coming from the wagon, Foxx added to the confusion among the attacking force by beginning a rapid-fire hail of rifle slugs. He snapped off his shots now, more interested in the volume of lead he could throw into the fray than in the accuracy of his aim.

Under fire from the mysterious vehicle in front of them and from Foxx in their rear, Apaches and renegades alike spurred their mounts in panic and fled from the field. Foxx looked for Lita again, but she was no longer lying where she'd fallen. He could not find her among the retreating horsemen, who dashed about in confusion.

For a short while the attackers milled aimlessly for a few moments until shouted commands brought them together near the place where they'd held their war council. They stopped and bunched up, turning to look at the wagon. For the moment Foxx and the mesa were ignored.

With ponderous slowness the wagon started to move again. It headed for the riders. They held their ground until rifle shots began spitting out of the walls of the approaching vehicle. Then they retreated, still afraid of the unknown. They wheeled and in a straggling line streamed south into the broken foothills.

Foxx watched the retreat until the last of the riders was out of sight, then turned his eyes to the wagon. It had stopped now, and men were clambering over its sides. As they dropped to the ground, Foxx blinked. He did not quite credit what he saw, but there was no mistaking Pepper's stocky figure. The feisty little man looked as cocky as ever, standing with his bowed legs spread, looking around at the scattered, sprawled forms of horses and men and the two or three riderless horses wandering aimlessly over what had narrowly missed becoming a battlefield.

Foxx cupped his hands around his mouth. "Pepper!" he shouted.

Pepper looked up and waved jauntily. "Wondered who them red bastards was after," he called. "Didn't stop to think it might be you! Come on down! I guess the fracas is over with."

Foxx stopped long enough to gather up the piles of ammunition he'd so carefully prepared and to drop the shells into his saddlebags, then picked his way down the ridge and started for the wagon. Pepper came to meet him.

"Looks like you couldn't wait for me to get back to that castle place and give you a hand," he greeted Foxx. "How'd you manage to git out, anyhow?"

"Oh, I give 'em the slip," Foxx said, and before Pepper could begin asking for details, went on, "What in hell kind of shebang have you got here, anyhow?"

"It ain't much, when you come right down to it," Pepper replied. "Just a bunch of ties spiked on top of a wagon bed."

"It sure looked good to me." Foxx smiled. He dug out a stogie and lighted it. "How'd you come to scheme it up?"

"Well, if you want me to start from the first, I kept on moving all night after I got away from that castle. I seen some of them fellows take after me, but they never caught up."

"I could tell you was keeping ahead of 'em," Foxx said. "I dogged your trail when I got free, but Lita and her brother—"

"Hold on," Pepper broke in. "That's the monte-dealing girl from Hell on Wheels. What's she got to do with all this?"

"It's too long a story to start on now," Foxx replied. "Anyhow, when they caught up to me, I sorta had to forget about you and look out for my own skin. But I figured you was making out all right."

"Damn right, I was. I got back to the construction camp and begun figuring a way to go back and see if I could help you. I didn't look to get an invite just to walk into that castle, but right about then I seen a teamster starting up to the railhead with a load of ties, and all of a sudden it come to me."

"Worked real good, too." Foxx looked at the wagon-fort. "You done a lot of work in a little bit of time, Pepper."

"I didn't want you to get all nerved up, waiting too long. After me and Pat Riley figured out how to go about fixing what I'd dreamed up, I hurried the boys at the shop a little bit, and it only taken 'em about an hour to spike them ties on a wagon bed. While they was fixing the wagon, I talked to your railroad policemen, and they rounded up a few more men that wasn't afraid of a little scrap. The policemen didn't have enough rifles to go around, so I scrounged up a few shotguns for close-in fighting. Then all of us got on board, and we started out."

"You mean you were going to ride it all the way down to that canyon?" Foxx shook his head. "Well, I got to give you credit, Pepper. You ain't a man to give up easy."

"Never was. And old as I am, I don't aim to start giving up easy now either." Pepper took out his makings and started rolling a cornhusk cigarette. "Look here, Foxx, we was headed for that castle when we heard the ruckus over here and come to see if it was somebody needing help. Like I said, we didn't know it was you. Thing is, we're this far along, and we got the wagon and the men we'd need to do a good job. Are you of a mind to go on and clear out that bunch we tangled with?"

Foxx shook his head. "Not now, Pepper. I've found out that Victorio's on his way here with a big bunch of his wild Apaches. For all I know, they've already got here. They're aiming to stop that bridge over the Santa Maria River."

"How'd you find that out?"

"Asking questions and listening. But what our job

is right now is to get that wagon up to where the bridge gang's working."

"That oughta not be too big of a job," Pepper said. "Once you get the damn thing rolling, it moves along pretty good."

"Let's get it rolling, then," Foxx said. "I don't know how many men Victorio's got, but I know the C&K ain't got no army to fight 'em with. You and me'll pretty much have to be the army, Pepper, and the way it looks right now, we're going to be heading into one hell of a big scrap!"

"Damn it all, Foxx, this is costing the C&K a lot of money!" Pat Riley said, looking down along the rocky canyon at the point where the railroad bridge was being built over the Santa Maria River. "We've been waiting four days now for Victorio's Apaches to show up, and so far we haven't seen hide nor hair of them! You sure they're heading this way at all?"

"Sure enough to bet the road's money on it," Foxx replied. "Don't forget, I seen a little handful of 'em in that scrap I was having when Pepper and the wagon happened by."

"Sure. But maybe losing out at that fight made Victorio change his mind about joining up with the night riders."

"Don't put your money on that idea, Pat," Foxx advised the construction superintendent. It's more a case of the night riders joining up with Victorio, the way I read it. And look at all the trouble they stirred up for the C&K, less'n a dozen of 'em."

"Oh, I suppose you're right," Riley agreed. "I just

don't see how the C&K comes into it so much, though."

"It's all part and parcel of one big scheme," Foxx said. "And that scheme won't work out if this line goes on east, to where the army can use it to get troops here in a hurry."

"I know that's what you told me," Riley said. "But this business about the Apaches running all the white folks out of a big chunk of Arizona Territory sure seems to me like it's pretty farfetched."

"So was a lot of other crazy schemes," Foxx pointed out. "I don't guess King George looked for anything to come out of a little bunch of colonies kicking up their heels a hundred years ago, and old John Brown was sure as hell crazy, but him and twenty men started the last big war when he tried to run some Federal agents out of Harper's Ferry."

Slowly Riley nodded his head. "I guess you've made your point," he told Foxx. "I'd sure like to see those army troops I wired for when you told me about all this."

"Give 'em time, Pat. It don't make much difference whether they send men from Fort Whipple or Fort Mohave, they'd have about the same distance to travel, almost two hundred miles. In Arizona Territory everyplace is a damn long way from anyplace else."

"You don't have to tell me that, Foxx."

"Even if the troops had moved out the same day you sent your telegrams, which you and me both know don't happen, they couldn't make it here for another two or three days," Foxx went on. "That's one reason why Victorio and the ones working with him don't want the C&K to get across this river."

"I'm getting edgy waiting," Riley said. "Maybe if I go back and try to get some of my work done, I'll get over it."

After the construction superintendent had gone back to the temporary office he'd set up at the bridgehead, Foxx lighted a stogie and studied the spot his improvised forces would have to defend when the Apaches struck. It was not, he knew, going to be a quick or an easy fight. The bridgehead and the work area behind it were not extensive, but the terrain on the downstream side of the bridge was rough and broken, which made the Apache attack almost impossible to detect in advance.

Before the night riders had begun their raids, the bridge construction crew had planned to have the span ready when the faster-moving tracklaying gangs reached the river with the rails. At the spot where the bridge would cross, a lip of rock arced out over a narrow canyon. On both sides the foundation piers for the span had been completed, and on the side where Foxx stood, the trestle underpinning that would support the trusses had been almost completed.

Jutting out over the canyon, the ends of the huge beams stopped in midair almost a hundred feet above the west bank of the river. Below the ends of the beams the river flowed, deep and turbulent, as it did the whole length of the five-mile canyon. Even though the Apaches were armed with guns, they still used fire arrows in their raids, and Foxx did not like to think of what a half-dozen of those flaming missiles would do to the creosote-soaked wooden beams. It would not be easy, he thought, to keep the Apaches far enough away to prevent them from using fire arrows.

Tossing the butt of his stogie into the canyon, Foxx watched it tumble until it splashed into the river. He walked back over the smoothed rock surface of the overhang until he reached the point where the bridge construction ended, and picked his way down the already graded right-of-way to Pepper's fortress-wagon. A half-dozen men were lounging under the wagon; it was the only shady spot that Foxx could see anywhere near by. Halloran, one of Jim Flaherty's railroad policemen, was leaning against the end of the wagon, looking out at the rough, jagged humps of the Hualapai foothills which stretched to the south.

"Anything happening?" Foxx asked.

"Nothing more than there has been," Halloran replied. "I tell you, Mr. Foxx, I'd sure rather be in a fight than have to sit around as long as we have, waiting for this one to start."

On getting back to the construction camp after the fight on the mesa, Foxx had taken Pat Riley aside and explained the trouble that was brewing. He'd explained the need for having a group of well-armed men who were willing to fight, men who would be standing ready at all times, and presented Riley with two alternatives: Riley could pick them from the C&K crews, men whom they knew, or Foxx would recruit them from the Hell on Wheels hangers-on.

Riley hadn't needed to think the matter over. He'd joined Foxx in selecting twenty men—all they could provide with rifles from the C&K's stores at La Paz and the construction camp and the railhead—who were now on regular schedules, some as sentries, others as one-man patrols watching the routes Victorio's Apaches could be expected to follow when they came up from the hacienda to attack the bridgehead. With Pepper as his second-in-command, and Flaherty's three railroad policemen, Foxx had a total force of twenty-five—including himself—to stand off the expected Apache assault.

"Waiting's the toughest part of it," Foxx agreed. He dropped his voice and asked, "How're the men off the track gangs standing up to it? Are they getting edgy, too?"

"Just look under the wagon," Halloran said. "You can see none of 'em seems to be bothered too bad. But I'd say all of us feel pretty much the same way. If there's going to be a fight, we'd like to see it start so we can get it over with."

"If I could speed things up, Halloran, I sure would." Foxx grinned. "But I imagine Victorio and his Apaches are moving about as fast as they can. I don't look for 'em to disappoint us."

"Don't worry," Halloran said. "I think most of our men have put in some kind of a hitch in the army. They won't turn out to be hayfeet, Mr. Foxx."

"Where's Pepper?" Foxx asked. "I can't keep track of him anymore. He's always prowling around when he's supposed to be sleeping, and when I look for him to be out prowling, I'll find him in one of the bunkhouse cars."

"He started down to the river about fifteen or twenty minutes ago. Said he was looking for O'Shea. He wanted to tell him something."

"I'll go look for him, then. I need to stretch my legs."

Lighting a stogie as he walked, Foxx started up the slope that led to the area the man patrolling south of the camp was assigned to cover. The ground was well trodden, with plenty of fresh prints made since the patrols had been started, but Foxx had no trouble identifying Pepper's boot prints. The little man's bowed legs distributed his weight unevenly, and the outside edges of his boot soles cut a bit more deeply into the soil.

In this area along the Santa Maria River the vegetation was scanty; only a few isolated patches of sage and greasewood swayed gently in an almost imperceptible breeze. To the north of the river the humped Hualapai foothills rose, hiding much of the terrain beyond them. Close to the riverbank, where Foxx now walked, the rock that formed the canyon surfaced frequently; only narrow strips of mud between the rocky outcroppings held signs of the passage of man or animals.

His mind occupied with the problems he faced in defending the unfinished bridge, Foxx puffed abstractedly on his half-smoked stogie as he walked along. He followed Pepper's footprints by glancing at the ground only when his own feet signaled him that the baked earth over which he walked was soft enough to hold a print. He snapped to alert vigilance instantly, though, when he reached the end of a rock outcropping and automatically glanced down to make sure he had not gotten off the trail. The mark left by one of Pepper's boots was there in the sandy soil, but superimposed on it was the hazy-edged imprint of an Apache moccasin.

Foxx's first reaction was to drop his stogie and grind its butt into the dirt to prevent the aroma of its smoke from betraying his presence. He bent over the prints to study them more closely.

A fine, thin rim of dry soil ran around the edge of the boot print where the moccasin had not overlapped it. Foxx's Comanche teachers had taught him that such a rim would last only minutes on the arid earth before crumbling, even in a breeze as light as the one which had begun to blow shortly after noon. Pepper must be very close to him indeed, Foxx thought, and the Apache who was stalking him would be still closer.

His hand was on the butt of his Smith & Wesson before Foxx realized it would be a mistake to use the gun. The presence of one Apache meant that there were others close enough to hear a shot. Foxx let go of the S&W's butt and unsheathed his knife. He moved ahead, dividing his attention between the sagebrush-dotted stretch just before him and the footprints on the ground.

Moving silently was another of the arts instilled in Foxx by stern Comanche teachers, and the skill learned in youth had in time come to be instinctive. He passed through the few clumps of sage without a twig brushing against him, and when he planted his feet on the ground, he did so with no crunching of dry sand.

Foxx saw Pepper before he spotted the Apache. The feisty little man was crouched over in a scanty clump of sage, his hat pushed back on his head, his eyes fixed in front of him. Foxx could not see what Pepper was watching, and did not try to, for he was concentrating on locating the Apache.

A greasewood shrub swaying against the wind drew Foxx's eye at once. The shrub was only a few yards ahead of him and a bit to his right. Foxx half-turned his body without moving his feet, to be facing the spot squarely. He'd just completed his half-turn when the Apache stalker rose. The Indian wore a holstered pistol and carried a rifle slung across his shoulders, but he had a stubby Apache bow in his hands. An arrow was already nocked and the bowstring drawn taut when the Apache stood up.

Foxx's Bowie knife had not been designed for throwing; it was a weapon fashioned for hand-to-hand combat. Foxx had no choice, though. He shifted his hand on the hilt to a throwing hold and spun the knife with a quick snap. It struck a split second before the Apache released his arrow, and the shaft sailed over Pepper's head as the Apache crumpled slowly to the ground, blood beginning to seep from his throat where Foxx's knife was buried.

Pepper whirled, his hand clawing for the butt of his revolver. He saw Foxx as he drew, and looked around for the source of the arrow.

"You don't need to worry, Pepper," Foxx said calmly. "I seen the Apache before he seen me. He's laying over there by that greasewood bush. That about makes us even, I'd say."

"This ain't no time for keeping scores," Pepper told Foxx impatiently. "Sneak up here by me as quiet as you snuck up on that Apache bastard. I got something to show you."

Foxx joined Pepper, who pointed to a fissure in the stone formation that stretched along the riverbank. He saw nothing for a moment; then a breechclout-clad figure passed the narrow slit. Pepper motioned for Foxx to remain motionless, and in a few seconds a second Apache passed the crack in the rock.

Keeping his voice low, Pepper said, "I been watching 'em sneak up for the last ten minutes. It's Victorio and his men, Foxx. They're getting ready to jump the bridgehead camp."

CHAPTER 16

Foxx watched the fissure while another Apache passed by, and still another. He asked Pepper, "How many of 'em have you counted?"

"Damn it, Foxx, I ain't been keeping count! I'd say I seen about thirty, give or take a few. And they're still going past." Pepper jerked a thumb toward the cleft in the stone as the figure of another Apache warrior glided by it.

"It's Victorio, right enough," Foxx said. "All right, Pepper, we've seen enough. Let's get back from the bank a ways, where we can talk."

Foxx stopped at the body of the Apache long enough to jerk his knife out of the man's neck and clean the blade by plunging it into the sand several times. Then he and Pepper moved quietly away from the riverbank, to another patch of sagebrush. They squatted down among the gray-green foliage, out of sight of the moving Apaches.

"What d'you figure, Foxx?" Pepper asked. "Will they hit us this evening, or wait till early in the morning?"

"I'd bet they'll do what the Apaches like best," Foxx replied. "It'll be the middle of the afternoon before they all get together under that bridgehead. They'll move early enough to finish their fight by sunset and sneak away soon as it's dark." He paused long enough to touch a match to a stogie. "How many men you got prowling down along the river?"

"Three. There's Stidham and Perkins and—"

"Never mind their names. You know about where to find 'em?"

"Pretty close. You want me to round 'em up?"

"As fast as you can. There's likely to be some more Apaches looking out for our patrols. Let's don't lose any more men than we can help. If Victorio's got as many men as he's supposed to, we're going to need all of ours."

"I'll start right now, then," Pepper said. "It'll be maybe an hour or so till I can find 'em and get 'em up to the bridge."

"That's good enough. Don't do any shooting unless you've got to. We've got the edge right now, but it'll be gone if they know we've spotted 'em."

Pepper nodded and started south, keeping low as he ran between the sparse patches of vegetation. Foxx watched him for a few minutes, then went on down the slope to the wagon.

"Send one of your men up to the bunkhouse car," he told Halloran. "Rouse the men on night patrol, and get 'em down here quick as you can. Better have him get Pat Riley, too. Looks like the Apaches finally got here. They're moving up now along the river. It'll be maybe two hours before they'll hit us."

Halloran wanted to hear more details, but Foxx cut him short. He mounted the graded roadbed and used the foundation piers and massive timbers of the truss underpinning for cover as he worked his way over the top of the rock arch until he could look down into the river valley.

For a moment Foxx didn't believe the evidence of his eyes. There were no Apaches in sight anywhere along the bank. He blinked and started to stand up, but a flick of motion caught his attention a short distance downstream. Foxx froze and watched for the motion to be repeated.

Then he saw the bronzed body of an Apache warrior, the hue of his skin making him almost invisible against the reddish stone wall. The man was making his way upstream toward the unfinished bridge, still a hundred yards away from where he was, by edging along a ledge so narrow that no one could have imagined that it would give even a mountain goat a toehold.

Foxx watched the man until he was hidden by the top of the beams, and understood. Victorio's warriors were assembling directly under his feet, using the jutting arch of stone which overhung the bank to cover them.

After he'd watched a dozen or more of the Apaches make their careful way along the ledge, Foxx sat down on one of the foundation piers and leaned back against the timber. He remembered quite well the riverbank formations on both sides of the bridgehead. Downstream the rock wall of the canyon rose in a sheer sweep, almost vertical, a rise that would be impossible to scale. A short distance upstream the solid rock face was broken by a wide sloping gravel bed that could be mounted at a run, and in very little time.

Foxx nodded and said thoughtfully to himself, "That's where Victorio's bound to bring his men up. He'd figure we won't be looking for them to come down from the north, and if it hadn't been for Pepper spotting 'em, we wouldn't have."

No elaborate defense plan was really needed, Foxx decided. Even though his force was outnumbered three or four to one by the Apaches, the element of surprise on which Victorio had counted would be lost. All that the defenders had to do was to station themselves north of the bridgehead and take the Indians as they came up the graveled slope leading from the river.

Satisfied that he'd solved his problem, Foxx returned to the wagon and gave Halloran his orders.

Less than an hour later Foxx stood at the top of the sloping gravel bed, his Winchester cradled in the crook of his elbow, and checked over the defenses. His slim force was posted at intervals along the top of the slope, with instructions to hold its fire until the Apaches were halfway up the rise. Foxx turned to Pat Riley, who'd been tagging along, watching.

"All we got to do now is wait, Pat," he said. "It ain't but a little while till sundown, and I figure Victorio won't wait till it gets plumb dark before he moves. Apaches need light to shoot by, the same as white men do."

"I hope you're right, Foxx," Riley said. "You

know, all I want is to get this thing settled, so my men can quit playing soldiers and get back to work on the bridge. We're running too far behind schedule as it is."

"Well, you ain't going to get no work done as long as there's Apaches and night riders dogging you all the time. You can't do much more than take things the way they come."

"That's what I keep telling myself," Riley replied. But it's sure hard sometimes. I know how bad Caleb wants—"

A shout from the right-of-way interrupted him. He and Foxx turned in time to see the storekeeper, his face grimed with soot, a bloody gash in his forehead, running toward them.

"Pat!" the man shouted as he saw Riley. "Apaches are up at the camp! They've set fire to my supply dumps!"

"Oh, Jesus God!" Riley gasped. "That'll be all we need, to have our materials burned!"

"We didn't have guns to fight them with," the storekeeper went on. "Every gun I had in my storeroom's down here!"

Riley turned to Foxx. "I'll have to pull my men off this job, Foxx. They'll be needed to put out the fire!"

"They're needed here to stop the Apaches!" Foxx retorted. "That fire means Victorio's ready to move! No, Pat! Not one man is going to leave his place here!" He asked the storekeeper, "How many Apaches did you see?"

"Only three or four, but there's bound to be more than that up by the dumps."

Foxx tossed his Winchester to Riley. "Come on,

Pat. Likely there wasn't more'n a half-dozen Apaches sent to set them fires, and I'm betting they're gone by now. If they're not, you and me can take care of 'em!"

At a dead run Foxx and Riley headed for the dumps. They saw the smoke rising as they got to the right-of-way grade, and disappearing into the humped foothills they saw the running figures of several Apaches. There were men milling around the burning heaps of rope, stacks of ties and timbers, tiers of crates and boxes and barrels. They were beating at the flames with gunnysacks and shoveling sand on the smoldering lumber piles, and Foxx could see quickly that there were no more Apaches in the area.

"There goes the damned Apaches!" Foxx called to Riley. "You won't have to worry about them any longer."

"I've got enough to worry about the way it is," Riley told him. "But if we can save the timber for the trusses, the rest of the stuff can burn without hurting us too much!"

"You'll do more good here than you will at the river, then," Foxx said. "That's the only place there'll be any more fighting, and I better get back there."

Even as Foxx spoke, a scattered volley of shots sounded from the stream. Riley handed Foxx the Winchester. "Go on. And good luck. Let's get this damn thing finished, once and for all!"

As Foxx started running back to the gravel bed, the firing rose to a crescendo. By the time he was halfway there, it had diminished in intensity, and when he reached the edge of the slope, only a few scattered shots were being fired. A handful of

Apaches had found cover along the water's edge and were keeping the railroad men pinned down.

Hearing the whistle of lead above his head, Foxx dropped to the ground and belly-crawled along the line of defenders until he found Halloran.

"We stopped 'em the first time," Halloran said when Foxx joined him. "Didn't lose a man either. They weren't expecting us to be here and ready."

"All we need to do is hold on awhile," Foxx told him. "If we shut 'em down here, there's no way they can get downstream except to swim. If they try to use the path they come up on, we can pick 'em off one at a time, and Victorio'll know it."

"We'll hold 'em," Halloran promised.

"See you do." Foxx nodded. "I'm going to scout around. You don't need me here right now."

Crab-crawling until he was out of the danger zone, Foxx went up on the grade and looked back at the supply dump. No flames were visible now, but a cloud of smoke hung over the area, and here and there men were beating at sparks that smoldered on some of the heaps. Foxx was still standing looking at the results of the Apache foray when Pepper and the men who'd been on patrol duty downstream from the bridge came panting up.

"Now, damn it, Foxx!" Pepper exclaimed as soon as he was close enough to make himself heard. "How come you got this fracas started before we got back here to help?"

"You'll have to go down to the river and talk to Victorio about that," Foxx told him. "He started it when he was ready—he sure didn't ask me whether it was all right or not."

"Well, now I'm here, let's go ahead with it," Pepper said cheerfully. "Where you want me and these fellows to be?"

"You men go over on the other side of the right-of-way and tell Halloran to put you where he needs you," Foxx told the three who'd returned with Pepper. "Pepper, you come along with me. I want to have a look-see down under that bridgehead."

"What kind of scheme you hatching up now?" Pepper asked as they started for the bridgehead. "You know them Apaches is holed up down there already. What good's it going to do you just to look at 'em?"

"Daylight ain't going to last forever," Foxx pointed out. "If we don't do something real fast, them Apaches will just melt away as soon as it's dark. We got to hit 'em good while we can get at 'em, Pepper, and stop this foolishness once and for all."

They walked out across the rock ledge, and Foxx lay down at its edge. "Hold my feet, Pepper," he said. "I'll see what it's like down there where Victorio and his men are holed up."

Inch by inch Foxx pulled himself forward until half his body was hanging in midair. The end of the ledge where the stonemasons had squared it off when setting the foundation piers was too deep, and he could not see the area beneath it. He signaled for Pepper to pull him back.

On the rock shelf Foxx told Pepper of the problem and pointed to the massive underpinning that stuck out several feet beyond the end of the shelf. "Let's try out at the end of one of them timbers," he suggested. "Maybe they'll get me far enough out so's I can see the riverbank."

Hanging over the end of the timber, with Pepper holding his ankles, Foxx found that he could see most of the area below the protruding ledge. It arced like a vaulted ceiling, leaving a wide shelf between its back wall and the river. The Apaches were huddled on the ledge, packed in so tightly that only inches were left between the men closest to the river and the swiftly swirling current. The entire area was in deep shadow, so Foxx did not try to make an accurate count, but he estimated that there were seventy or eighty warriors.

Unmistakable amid the bare torsos of the Apaches were the renegades from the hacienda. Among them Foxx glimpsed a tan charro jacket embroidered in gold, but so many moving bodies obstructed his view that he could not tell whether the wearer was Lita or Pino. He leaned farther forward, trying to get a better angle of view, and one of the Apaches looked up and saw him.

Foxx noticed the upturned brown face just in time. "Pull me up quick!" he called to Pepper, getting the words out an instant before the Apache's shout of discovery.

He felt Pepper pulling at his legs and swung his body to help start some momentum. His head cleared the bottom of the big underpinning timbers just in time. Seconds after Foxx's belt scraped over the timber's edge, he heard the thunking of Apache rifle bullets driving into it from below.

"They're there, like I figured," Foxx told Pepper. "Packed so tight a man wouldn't have to aim. If we could just figure a way to get at 'em from up here, it'd be like shooting fish in a rainwater barrel." He looked down the side of the cliff's face. On both sides of the ledge it was a sheer vertical wall of solid stone, without a crevice to provide a footrest or handhold.

"A man'd have to be a spider to crawl down that," Pepper said, discouragement in his voice.

"Hold up, Pepper," Foxx broke in. "You called the turn. You ever watch a spider run down on its web?"

"Sure, but—" Pepper paused, and his face brightened. "I see what you're driving at, Foxx. We'll let ourselves down the sides there on ropes!"

"We'll have somebody up here let us down," Foxx corrected him. "That'll leave our hands free. We'll brace our feet on the side, lean out and shoot, and pop outa the way behind the edge before they can shoot back."

"I'm game if you are," Pepper agreed. "Where's the rope coming from, though?"

"There's miles of it at the supply dump. Men to hold it, too. You wait here and keep an eye on the Apaches. I'll be back in a minute."

Foxx hurried to the supply dump. The fires were all out by now, and most of the smoke had drifted away. Only a few thin threads rose from stacks of supplies that were still smoldering. He found a grimy-faced Pat Riley standing in the middle of a crowd of construction workers, whose soot-stained skin and clothing showed they'd been fighting the fires. Riley was looking across at what remained of the material that was to have been used in the new bridge.

"How bad was the fire, Pat?" Foxx asked.

"It could've been worse, I guess. We lost a lot of little stuff, but we saved the truss timbers. But that's not bothering me right now, Foxx. What happened to the Apaches?"

"We've got 'em pinned down under the rock ledge at the bridgehead. Let me have some rope, Pat. Me and Pepper's going to get some men to lower us down to where we can use our guns, and we'll give Victorio a lesson that'll keep him away from C&K property from here on out."

Riley looked at Foxx for a moment, a sad smile forming on his face. "Rope? That's one thing we're fresh out of."

"Hell, there was a couple of miles of it coiled up over—" Foxx turned to point and saw the fire-devastated supply yards. He asked Riley, "You mean it all burnt up?"

"Every last inch. So did all our harness straps. I'm sorry, Foxx, but that's the way it is."

"There's got to be something I can—" Foxx began, looking around the yards. His eyes fell on one of the men in the work gang; over his sweat-streaked shirt he wore a pair of bright new suspenders. So did the men standing on both sides of him. Foxx turned back to Riley. The superintendent also had on new suspenders of the same kind. Foxx had recognized them as the extra-wide, extra-heavy kind issued to the U.S. Cavalry.

"Ain't them cavalry galluses?" he asked Riley.

Riley's face showed his surprise at Foxx's unexpected question, but he said, "A peddler passed through with a wagonload of them a week or so ago. The place that makes them had a bunch the army didn't take. He was selling them for a dime, and I suppose every man on the job bought some."

"There's my rope, then." Foxx turned to the work gang. "Any of you men want to sell the C&K your suspenders for a dollar a pair?"

"You can sure buy mine!" one of them called.

"Mine, too!" another chimed in.

"Hell, I'll give you mine, just to get back at the Apaches!" a third volunteered. "I bought a spare pair, anyhow."

With the storekeeper keeping track of his purchases, Foxx bought suspenders until the work crew ran out.

"Now I need some of you men for a sorta special job," Foxx said. "If you got a grudge against the Apaches, come along and work it off!"

With Riley and the storekeeper in the van, the entire crew followed Foxx back to the bridgehead. With the help of the work gang the suspenders were quickly knotted together to make two stout but stretchy ropes.

"I'm ready to go if you are, Pepper," Foxx said.

"Any time you say." Pepper had a cornhusk cigarette hanging from his lips. He spat it out and picked up his rifle. "Like you said awhile back, daylight ain't going to last forever."

Foxx waited until he saw Pepper start down the face of the cliff, then girded the other rope around his hips and with three men anchoring him at the top started over the side.

He found it easier going than he'd expected. The springy elastic of the suspenders absorbed the sudden tugs he gave as he leaned out and walked backward down the cliff. He reached the point where the masons had faired their vertical cutaway of the arch into the main cliff and signaled his anchormen to stop. Dangling in midair, his feet planted firmly, he leaned sideways and peered into the deep, gloomy niche.

There had been little change since his last reconnaissance. The Apache warriors were packed shoulder to shoulder on the wide ledge, waiting stoically for their leader to tell them what to do next. They did not notice Foxx, high above their heads. Foxx waited until he saw Pepper's head silhouetted against the rim of the arch on the opposite side. He nodded and waited until he could see that Pepper was leveling his rifle into the packed mass, then began triggering his Winchester.

Like repeated thunderclaps the shots echoed and reechoed in the dimness of the recess. The Apaches started milling about, like ants whose hill had been stirred up.

When the warriors around them started falling, many of the Apaches tried to press deeper into the niche. A number of them ran for the wide path leading to the graveled incline up which they'd started their attack. Foxx heard the sharp barking of shots as Halloran's men began picking off the warriors trying to use the only real path out of what had turned into a trap.

Those of Victorio's men who kept their wits looked for the source of the shooting, but the echoes made the origin of the rifle blasts difficult to pinpoint. Many of them stood staring across the river, trying to spot attackers on the opposite bank. Only a few were quick to locate Foxx and Pepper. These brought up their rifles, but the jostling of their companions made accurate shooting impossible; their bullets glanced off the curved surface of the overhanging arch and spattered into the river.

Foxx emptied the Winchester's magazine and swung around the rim, to shelter behind the overhang while he reloaded. He saw heads beginning to appear on the surface of the river as some of the Indians leaped in and began trying to swim to safety. When he looked again into the gloomy recess below, there were fewer Apaches, and those who had stayed were either packed tightly at the rear of the niche or standing ready to return the fire Foxx and Pepper had loosed on them.

Foxx saw a pair of charro jackets, gold embroidery glinting in the dimness, and as his eyes grew accustomed to the lessened light, was able to distinguish Lita from Pino. They stood near the edge, the river at their feet. Lita was facing Foxx, Pino had his back turned. Lita saw Foxx's head and shoulders silhouetted against the sky. She raised her rifle, but Foxx had his Winchester leveled and was squeezing off a shot while she was still bringing her weapon to her shoulder.

She pushed Pino with the barrel of the rifle to get him out of her way. Pino lost his balance and swayed. Foxx's slug took him in the shoulder. Pino grabbed his sister's arm as his legs started to give way, and as he toppled into the river, he pulled Lita in with him. Foxx emptied the Winchester's magazine and swung around to the cliff. He watched the river for several minutes, but the son and daughter of Mangas Coloradas remained hidden in its swift green depths.

On the other side of the niche Pepper had continued firing. Foxx resumed, too, and more Apache warriors fell. A high-pitched voice shouted a command in Apache. Foxx did not understand the words—the Comanche and Apache languages came from different rootstocks—but the intonation was unmistakable. The Apache warriors responded quickly. They crowded to the bank of the river and began jumping in. The surface of the water was covered with bobbing heads. Now and then one of the heads disappeared below the water and did not return to the surface.

Foxx watched the devastating retreat impassively. He felt no need to gloat or to rejoice, but he was certain that a long time would pass before Victorio or any other Apache war chief again attacked any property belonging to the C&K Railroad.

"I just don't understand it," Caleb Petersen told Foxx. The president of the C&K was sitting at the dinner table in his private car in the C&K yards at La Paz. Foxx sat across the table, Vida Martin between him and Caleb on one side, Clara Petersen on the other. "I'm disappointed, of course. I put all the faith in the world in Frank Sanders."

"There's not any way to get around the evidence, Caleb," Foxx said quietly. "After things settled down at the bridgehead and the track gangs got back pushing iron on schedule, the first thing I done was to have a private look at Sanders's office. I had to wire Jim Flaherty to get the combination of the safe, and then I picked some locks on the inside compartments. But you seen what I found."

"Who do you think Sanders sold out to, Foxx?" Caleb asked.

"That's the one thing he never put on paper," Foxx replied. "Everything else was there. But you know who's trying to beat us out, on the north and on the south. Now if you want me to, I'll look both ways and come up with the answer."

After a moment of thoughtful silence Caleb shook his head. "No. I don't think I want you to. When we got to Ocampo, and Sanders wasn't there to meet us, I knew something was wrong. Then I got that insulting answer from President Diaz when I wired him to confirm the meeting that Sanders was supposed to have arranged but didn't, and I knew that I'd better get back here in a hurry. I didn't know how bad it was until I heard what you had to report. But I think the best thing we can do is forget about the whole sorry episode."

"Don't you think Caleb is right, Foxx?" Clara Petersen asked anxiously. "Vida and I both do."

Foxx took a sip from the glass of Cyrus Noble he held before he replied, "I ain't so sure I'd want to forget it. When somebody you've trusted puts a knife in your back, you want to remember it, or you're likely to get stabbed again." He looked at Caleb and added, "But if you mean you don't want it talked about, I'd say you're right. Whoever bought Sanders won't talk, because they know the C&K won in spite of their dirty tricks."

Later, after everyone had retired, when Caleb and Clara were certain to be asleep, Vida Martin slipped from her stateroom into the one occupied by Foxx. When they had greeted one another in a prolonged and satisfying fashion, Vida propped herself up on an elbow and looked at Foxx in the dim light of the stateroom.

"Was I wrong," she asked, "or did I catch a hint of personal experience in the way you answered Caleb? Did somebody you'd trusted stab you in the back while I was gone, Foxx?"

"I don't rightly follow you."

"I was thinking about that girl you mentioned, Mangas Coloradas's daughter. She sounded like a hellcat to me, a real vixen."

"Would it make any difference in the way you feel about me?"

"No. We've always agreed, no strings, no questions. And I don't want to change that. It's a good, honest way to live."

"I'll tell you the whole story, if you want me to," Foxx offered.

"I don't think I do." Vida snuggled close to him and whispered, "And truly, I don't begrudge you. I think it's a law of nature that some time or other in his life every fox must have a vixen."

"Gruesomely effective.
A scary, engrossing book."
—Stephen King,
author of *Firestarter*

The Unforgiven
by Patricia J. MacDonald

Maggie tried to forget the body of the man she loved, the murder trial, and the agonizing punishment. Now she was free to start a new life on a quiet New England island—until the terror began again.

"A terrific psychological thriller." —Mary Higgins Clark, author of *The Cradle Will Fall*

"...one of those rare books that, once started, you can't put down." —John Saul, author of *When the Wind Blows*

A Dell Book   **$3.50**   **(19123-8)**

At your local bookstore or use this handy coupon for ordering:

| Dell | DELL BOOKS   THE UNFORGIVEN $3.50   (19123-8)
P.O. BOX 1000, PINE BROOK, N.J. 07058-1000 |

Please send me the above title. I am enclosing $_____ (please add 75c per copy to cover postage and handling). Send check or money order—no cash or C.O.D.'s. Please allow up to 8 weeks for shipment.

Mr./Mrs./Miss_____

Address_____

City_____State/Zip_____